For Kenzie

CHAPTER 1

LONDON, SPRING 1935

The curse of a great city is in its circulatory system — those veins of traffic, those arteries of tube stops — all it takes is one blockage and the body shuts down.

The tracks behind the railway station were swarming with officers this morning. The area was being cordoned off, marking the recent troubles, and the irate public pressed against the bobbies assigned to keep them at bay, like ocean waves heaving against anchored buoys.

My dark felt hat pulled low over my brow, I manoeuvred my way through this crowd, targeting a member of the constabulary who would let me through the cordon. My chosen profession required that I move incognito amongst the general population. Witnesses and criminals had a way of making themselves scarce around detectives. There were several photos of me in local newspapers, but they didn't look anything like me, and that was quite on purpose. "P.C. Adams the detective" was an elaborate costume I wore to make an impression, regalia that consisted of high heels, artful makeup, and expensive clothing.

By comparison, Portia Adams, my true self, was totally forgettable. Today I wore my father's old threadbare coat and my lowest-heeled boots. My shoulder-length hair was pinned up in a bun under my hat. It would be hard to mistake me for the celebrity P.C. Adams. Unless you knew me.

"Ma'am, you'll have to step back," said the deep voice of Constable Perkins before he realized who he was talking to. "Blimey! Miss Adams, didn't recognize you there."

He extended his gloved hand my way to guide me through the cordon, ignoring the protests of the people around us.

"Sergeant Michaels called for you, eh?" Perkins said, pointing to where the rotund officer could be seen puffing away at a cigar. "Figures. It's an odd one."

"My favourite," I answered with a smile his way. I picked my way through the snow — unexpectedly deep at this time of year — and headed in the direction he had pointed, dodging the melee of police and firemen. My eyes were everywhere: the tracks, the rubbish strewn about, the snow, the disturbance of the snow, the myriad of footprints. All of it could be relevant. I pulled out my belated Christmas gift from my grandfather, a new Contax camera. It had been delivered a few days ago and had included a note of apology for his absence. Sherlock Holmes remained abroad, travelling the Indian subcontinent, and no doubt causing trouble wherever he went.

I grinned, thinking of my grandfather, covering my inappropriate facial expression with my camera as I snapped several landscape shots of the full scene, turning back to take a few of the police cordon, and then one of Sergeant Michaels.

"Make sure'n get that lazy drunk sobered up, Rourke," Michaels barked at one of his constables, his open winter coat flapping in the wind like the wings of a large bat. The constable was escorting a scrawny man who seemed to be having trouble putting one foot in front of the other.

"Adams," he said by way of greeting.

"Inspector," I replied with a nod.

He froze at the mention of his new rank. His cigar threatened to fall out of his suddenly gaping mouth, but somehow managed to stay attached at the corner of his lip where it trembled precariously like a diver who couldn't quite make up her mind to take the plunge.

"Your uniform shirt is brand new," I answered before he could ask. "And it's been tailored, which none of your other shirts have been. You're hardly the type to visit a tailor for fashion reasons, but you would need their services in order to get the pips sewn onto your shirt. You're wearing your jacket, but I'd wager that if you took it off, we'd see your sergeant stripes very loosely stitched onto your new shirt — because they're about to be replaced, no doubt."

"It's not official yet, Adams," Michaels hissed at me, stepping close so no one would overhear. "Keep your Goddamned detecting down!"

"And yet it is my 'Goddamned detecting' you called me down here for."

"Bollocks. This here is what you'd call an educational opportunity," he replied, tapping his cigar with his ring finger so that the ashes fell in a neat grey pattern on the snow. "Better that you learn what you can from official sources rather than the ones closer to you and less legal if you know what I mean."

I did know what he meant. He was referring to my grandparents. But not Dr. and the first Mrs. Watson. Michaels was referring to my two living grandparents, Sherlock Holmes and Irene Adler. Neither of whom Michaels held in high regard. A yell from somewhere behind us gave me the excuse to move past it quickly. "I don't know what to say ..."

"Well, that's a flippin' first," he answered sarcastically, his eyes on the man being hauled away from the cordon. "But how about you start with 'thank you Sergeant Michaels for considering my further education'?"

I grimaced at his condescending words until he gave up waiting for my gratitude. The man who had caused the opportune disturbance gripped his picket sign in both hands, using it to beat back against the constables, his words railing against the king of England no less. That's a good way to arrange a cold evening in the basement of Scotland Yard. The problem was that the state of the pound and the resultant suffering of the British people meant that his words accurately reflected the current sentiment against the royal family. I scanned the crowd, picking out other signs, including a few for the Ship Builders Union and one for the Irish Feminist League.

"Go take a look at the scene, would you?" Michaels said, the cigar waggling back and forth at the corner of his mouth.

"The train jumped the tracks, that much is obvious," I replied, looking at the tracks, the position of the train, and up at the officers standing on the platform. "This morning, and quite early, before the rush hour of the morning commute."

"And how do you know that?" he prompted, hands in his coat pockets.

"The train had no rail cars and the snow has been falling steadily all morning, but hasn't covered the damaged train," I replied, pointing to the vehicle. "It was being moved into position to take on its cars."

I looked down the rail tracks in both directions — the ones leading to the platform and the ones leading back to the rail yard — and spied Annie trying to talk her way through the police cordon closely followed by an ancient photographer I recognized from *The Sunday Times*. The young blonde saw me looking and shook her head. I knew her well enough to recognize that her journalistic pride kept her from asking me to chaperone her around the crime scene, especially with a photographer in tow. I turned my attention back to Michaels. "But why did it leave the rail yard without its cars?"

"It was being moved into position to take on its cars when it accelerated in this direction," Michaels put in. "At least according to the damp squib who was drivin' it."

"So, it started in the rail yard, left the yard without its rail cars, and ran into this platform?"

"Looks that way, don't it?" he replied, stepping up the stairs that led to the platform to speak to one of his officers, his coat flapping around him comically. If the winds got much gustier, he would be able to fly back to Scotland Yard.

"But why?" I said aloud, running my hand along the track and looking back towards the rail yard where other trains stood in neat rows.

"Ice or speed?" Michaels called from where he stood.

"Irrelevant," I replied, though not loudly enough for him to hear. I had now walked away from the platform and was making my way along the east side of the tracks slowly, collecting and dismissing clues one by one.

I was halfway to the rail yard when Constable Bonhomme caught up to me, slightly out of breath, and presented me with a brake cable. "The sergeant said to show you this, Miss Adams. He said you can tell that the train was going too fast by the way this cable broke."

I examined the stripped cable. "Yes, I see, Bonhomme. Thank you. But it doesn't explain why the train was speeding, or even how he got up to that speed in time to jump the tracks and hit the platform."

"The driver — Harold Digby's his name — is in no condition to tell us how he did it," Bonhomme answered, backing up as I continued my careful examination of the rails at our feet. "Sergeant Michaels says between the drink and the crash, it'll be hours before he's of any use to us."

"He was drunk when the accident happened?" I asked, looking up from the ground for a moment and noticing the talc on Bonhomme's sleeve. Another new baby in the family, I confirmed, looking at his shoulder to where evidence of dried spit-up could be discerned if you were looking for it.

Bonhomme nodded. "If that'll be all, I should get this evidence back to the lorry."

My eyes flicked from the man at my side to where I could see Constable Brian Dawes speaking to Michaels on the platform. The tall man was too disciplined to wave, but he flashed me a quick grin when Michaels looked down at his notes for a second.

I grinned back like an idiot. There were a lot of ways in which my brain differed from those around me — especially when it came to my rigid focus on details — but when it came to attraction, I was a fool, just like every human before me.

Bonhomme ran between the tracks towards the platform, distracting me for a moment from Brian, and something about his large boot prints in the snow captured my attention — a wire had been revealed by his footsteps.

"What?" I whispered, recognizing the danger. "NO!" I yelled as loudly as I could, my eyes on the constable still running away from my position. "Bonhomme, get off the tracks!"

And then I was flying through the air, caught by the absolution of darkness.

CHAPTER 2

THE SMELL WAS THE first thing I remembered as I woke. Disinfectant. A salve of some kind. Mint? Softness pressing down on me. I tried to open my eyes. Too hard. Darkness.

I woke again to the same smell, only realizing that it was the second time because I remembered recognizing it before. Someone was prodding me with a needle. I tried to bat them away, but my arms felt as heavy as lead bars, as did my eyelids. Grey.

A hand shook me awake and a face that couldn't be here swam into my vision.

"Papa?" I mumbled, trying to sit up and realizing I was in my toddler bed back in Toronto.

"Sleep, chérie," he whispered. "It's late. We'll talk tomorrow."

But I knew we wouldn't talk tomorrow, or ever again. He would be critically wounded in a battle an ocean away from our little home and his loss would devastate my mother, my grandparents, and everyone who loved him.

Awake again. I strained my ears and heard nothing. The softness extended over my legs, but my feet felt cold. The smell was stronger now, closer. I faded out again with that thought in my head.

An explosion!

My eyes flew open this time, the lids feeling heavy and fixed after who knows how long of disuse.

Beside what I could now see was my hospital bed slept Annie Coleson and her twin brothers, their blonde heads on their chests, their breathing even.

I could barely turn my head to see them, and raising my hand painfully, I could feel why. The bandages all around my skull were thick and covered my forehead, ears, and back of my head.

I watched Annie's chest rise and fall, noticing the dark skin under her eyes and wondering how long she had been sitting vigil at my bedside. The twins looked better, but I'm sure they would have been more comfortable in their own beds at home. A quick assessment of Annie's clothes, her makeup, and the note-pad beside her told me they had been here a few hours at least. I felt a rush of love for my friend and would have expressed it had the darkness not stolen over me again.

I woke to a dull thudding sound. No, not thudding, I corrected, but drumming? I struggled to open my eyes, wincing at how dry they felt.

Through slit eyes I could see Annie, without her brothers this time, her mouth moving in rhythm with the drumming sound. That was not drumming, I realized, painfully squinting at her mouth. That was the sound of her voice! It was slightly higher pitched than the sound coming from a nurse she was speaking to. I could discern no actual words from either of them. It was like listening to a conversation while underwater. How thick were these bandages around my head?

"Annie," I tried to say, though it was hard to force my lips to move.

She heard me and gleefully pointed at me. She flew to my side, scooping up my hand and speaking rapid fire. At least, she seemed to be speaking quickly, judging from the movement of her lips; I still couldn't hear a word she was saying.

The nurse, meanwhile, had come to my other side and was fiddling with my iv.

"Annie," I said again, the fear starting to build in me as I wondered at my injuries. I couldn't even hear the words I was saying. "Thirsty …"

She frowned, stopping her drumming sounds for a beat before she shook her head and said something to the nurse.

The nurse leaned over and spoke directly at me, her deep drumming a little louder but no clearer.

I tried to shake my head, but shooting pain arched between my brows and I bit my lip to keep from crying out.

Annie's grip on my hand tightened and her mouth moved again, her eyes concerned. The nurse responded to whatever she said by taking my wrist in her hand again, her other hand holding a syringe.

I said, "No, please don't. The pain is bearable."

But though they both heard me (I could tell by the way they glanced at me and then each other) the drugs flowed unabated into my bloodstream. I fought against the fog and lost.

When I awoke this time it was morning — I could tell that even before I forced my eyelids open to see Brian at my bedside.

He smiled when I opened my eyes, his dimples reappearing as he called for someone over his shoulder. His voice was a slightly deeper drum sound than either Annie's or the nurse's.

Brian leaned over me holding a glass of water with a straw and I took a long thankful drink before speaking.

"Brian, it's so good to see you," I said as clearly as I could.

He got that confused look I was beginning to dread and grasped my hand, speaking urgently to me in that same dulled drum sound.

The fact that I couldn't hear might mean I was speaking too

quietly, so I repeated my earlier thanks, concentrating and trying to speak louder.

I still couldn't discern my own words. He jumped in response and I gripped Brian's hand, noticing that his left hand was bandaged. Surely he hadn't been caught in the explosion as well!

"What happened to your hand, Brian?" I asked, carefully lifting the hand that was holding mine.

Brian grimaced, looking from his hand to mine, still not understanding my words, but gently speaking in a softer drumming tone. I shook my head, the pain diminishing in direct opposition to my growing panic. Why couldn't we understand one another? How badly were my ears damaged? Had my vocal cords been hurt as well? I pulled at the bandages around my ears — how thick were they?

Brian grasped my hands to prevent me from pulling off the bandages and a doctor arrived carrying a dreaded hypodermic needle. I struggled against Brian even more. No! I needed to stay awake to figure out what was happening to me. It was my right!

"Stop!" I yelled as loud as I could, kicking the blankets off the bed. But even though I could tell they heard me by the surprise on their faces, the doctor pressed on, grabbing for my arm even as I fought.

Suddenly everyone stopped moving, their attention on the door. I only noticed because Brian's hand suddenly released mine, and I was struggling against nothing.

There in the doorway stood my grandmother, Irene Adler. I had never been so happy to see her.

She glanced at the men in the room, her drumming sound melodic to me even in my current state, but her eyes shot ice at the doctor. Whatever she said to him, he flushed and dropped my arm.

She waved my boyfriend out of the room with her cane, Brian's gaze lingering on me before he allowed himself to be driven out.

I would have asked him to stay had he been able to understand me, but I was proud of the way he met my grandmother's gaze defiantly before he nodded to her and left. Most people withered under her gaze.

"Thank God you're here," said I.

Her blue eyes widened at my words. She spoke back to me, causing me to shake my head, still not understanding a word and obviously not being understood.

The doctor, however, got a triumphant look on his narrow face, pointing at me like I was a defective lab rat and speaking to my grandmother as she stepped to my bed, putting her hand protectively on my bare ankle. The doctor was a gambler who frequented Bethnal Green, if his boxing chit was any indication, and I tried to dismiss him from my case on those grounds, but again, no one understood me.

They continued to speak to each other, all but ignoring me, and as angry as I was, I felt my mind refocus. Something had happened to my hearing, that much was very clear. Hopefully the damage was not permanent, but what could have happened to my speech? I could feel words coming out of my mouth, my tongue seemed functional, and I was able to make sound — that much was also clear by the reactions of the people around me. I ran my hands over my throat and found no bandages or injuries, and then did a visual assessment of my body now that it was no longer covered by blankets.

My hands and my head were bandaged, as was my right knee, but in bending it, I could tell it was not serious. I smelled singed hair, which made sense since I had been in an explosion, and that also probably accounted for the smell of salve coming from the bandages on my hands.

On the bed, the doctor had put down his clipboard and I eagerly scooped it up to read my health chart. They had diagnosed a concussion. Not severe, but enough of a blow to account for rendering me unconscious. My burns were very minor and they had not operated. They did not believe I had internal bleeding, but there had been swelling in my ear canals from the explosion. The last line of the diagnosis speculated about hearing loss, but nowhere on the page did it say anything that would explain the speech issues I was experiencing.

Flipping the chart over to a blank sheet, I carefully wrote a message, hoping that the fact that I could read also meant that I could still write. The brain was, after all, a curious organ that medical science did not fully understand. It was possible that hearing was connected to speech and that to lose one through physical damage affected the other. As far as I knew, though, an inability to communicate orally would not be connected to the ability to write.

I tugged on my grandmother's sleeve, interrupting what had become an escalating drumming sound that signalled a heated argument between her and the doctor.

Her eyes flew over the message I had written, "I cannot hear any of you. All I hear is a dull drumming sound, like a piano being played with the damper pedal pressed down."

Her eyes met mine and she nodded just once, decisively.

CHAPTER 3

USING A PENCIL AND paper took a great deal longer than speech, but at least I was able to communicate again.

My cousin, Dr. Hamish Watson, assigned himself as an adjunct doctor. Through him I learned that the explosion had ruptured both my eardrums and the concussion came from being thrown backwards and into a rail track. He told my grandmother that he had seen complete recoveries from such injuries during the war, but that it was also possible that I would never regain my full hearing. He wasn't sure what was affecting my speech, but he could see nothing physically wrong with my vocal cords or my tongue.

My grandmother wrote that recognizable words were coming out of my mouth, but that they were gibberish. I was able to form words, but the words I thought I was saying were not the words I was actually saying. We tested the phenomenon several times with me concentrating on saying my name and Watson as witness.

Every time I said "Portia Constance Adams" out loud, the words I actually said were different and seemingly random. Once I said "squirrel toast blue" and another attempt came out "spit old under." My grandmother wrote my words back to me as I said them and I could make no more sense of them than she could. We both looked to my cousin for a diagnosis or a treatment, my grandmother actually providing the question verbally.

I saw the answer in his body language before he finished writing; he didn't know. He wrote that the concussion I had suffered may have done damage to the part of my brain that controlled speech, but admitted that was pure speculation. His hope was that as my eardrums recovered, so too would the rest of my physical injuries. He was, however, going to consult with his brother and other doctors on my recovery plan. The Watsons had been very kind to me since I had inherited 221 Baker Street from our shared grandfather, Dr. John Watson, and this was just another demonstration of their love.

The newspapers covered the train yard bombing, and, upsettingly, referred to my injuries as "extreme problems of the mind" and "a serious blow to the detective of Baker Street." The London news even quoted a psychiatrist whom I'd never met, but who supposedly had assessed my symptoms as "insurmountable by a delicate female of my class." At least my condition was relegated to the bottom sections of the paper. The fervent criticism of the king and the government was splashed all over the front page. The photos of Queen Mary being shielded by her staff from rotten food being hurled her way, in this case by an older woman with a fierce look, were especially convincing that the British people had lost patience with their leaders.

But it was Inspector Michaels and Brian who delivered the worst news of all. Brian, who at this visit was exhibiting pale purple discoloration under his eyes, took the notebook to break the news that Constable Bonhomme had been killed and one other officer I didn't know by name had lost a leg in the blast.

Michaels puffed on a cigar by the door during this exchange, finally stepping forward as I shook my head in disbelief at this message.

He spoke, his drumming sound hesitant, and then, remembering my affliction, threw up his hands and waved towards Brian.

Brian wrote an explanation, "He's trying to apologize for calling you down to the rail yard. He's taking this all very hard. Especially losing Bonhomme."

I nodded. Of course he would. I wrote back, "Tell him I don't blame him, and I'm sure Bonhomme's family doesn't blame him either."

Brian showed the note to Michaels, who grunted in response, a sound I almost recognized despite my injuries.

I, in the meantime, wrote, "What happened to your hands? You weren't that close to the blast."

Brian took back the note, Michaels reading over his shoulder, and it was the inspector who took the paper away to scrawl, "You were on fire. Dawes put you out with his bare hands."

I glanced up at Brian incredulously.

"Michaels came a few seconds later with a blanket," Brian wrote, his face betraying how panicked he had felt in those moments and perhaps how silly he felt when Michaels appeared with the blanket. "The doctor says that your gloves and coat protected you while I have serious burns on my left hand."

I put my bandaged hand over his bandaged hand and tried to express my thanks that way. His eyes met mine and then he glanced away and winced. How much pain was he in?

"Wired bomb?" I wrote, watching Brian's face.

Michaels nodded brusquely over Brian's shoulder, a steady stream of drum sounds flowing out of his cigar-clamped mouth. Brian quickly wrote and handed me the note, "Yes. Bonhomme hit the trip wire."

I looked from the note to the men, surprise evident on my face, to which Michaels nodded grimly.

"Russian? From war?"

Brian wrote back, "Still identifying. Box 850 helping."

"Why didn't it go off as the train passed over the tracks?" I wrote.

Brian showed the note to the inspector, who said something Brian wrote down. "Train was wired too. Digby was passed out drunk on the floor of the train and never even woke until the train hit the platform. Intent was to blow up the train. Digby released."

I shook my head again. Who would wire a train to explode before it was in service? And what did Bonhomme do to that trip wire that a train did not? He was lighter by far … he must have literally pulled a wire free. Or maybe the snow had frozen the wire to the track.

"None of this makes sense," I wrote after a few moments' thought.

Michaels wrote back, "Get well fast and help us figure out what is going on before it happens again."

CHAPTER 4

A WEEK LATER THE nurses finally removed my bandages. Annie sat beside me as they did so, my grandmother standing behind the doctor. I watched Annie's face as the last of the bandages were unwound and the relief on her face helped my stomach unclench slightly.

She spoke to me and then Dr. Watson and my grandmother. They must have agreed to whatever she asked because as he used various instruments to peek into my ear, she pulled out her little pocket mirror.

Hesitating, she fumbled, writing a note on the ever-present pad on my lap, "Bruises heal and hair grows back." Only when I'd read it and nodded impatiently did she hand me the small round mirror.

She needn't have worried, the yellow and orange-coloured bruises around my eyes and cheeks didn't concern me at all and the few actual cuts on my face were minor and healing. My forehead looked reddened from the fire and my hair would need to be cut much shorter because of the burnt parts, but considering the fate of the others who had been hit by the blast, I had been lucky. Brian was in a lot of pain and his hands would bear the scars of fire for the rest of his life. And Bonhomme ...

Unfortunately, the removal of the bandages had made no

discernible difference to my hearing and I wrote a few lines for
Watson, asking what he had seen in my ears.

He stepped back to peer into my ear again before he spoke,
Annie transcribing, "Your ears are improving. The scabbing over
your eardrums has gone down. Are you noticing any improvement at all?"

I shook my head, having understood none of what he had
said aloud.

Watson shrugged and spoke again. Whatever he said got Annie
tearful and she shook her head several times. Annie wrote, "He
says it will take time to fully recover."

"Perhaps my hearing will return as my concussion improves,"
I muttered, shaking my head at Annie as she wiped away her
tears. It was gibberish anyway. Both my speaking of it and Watson's reassurances as far as I was concerned.

"I WISH YOU WOULD go to a private hospital. You would have
the best care and the finest doctors. The Watsons are adequate
physicians, but their side of your family tree is known for loyalty
and friendship, not brains."

It was just the elegant handwriting of my grandmother, but even
without the sound of her voice to punctuate it I knew her tone
was one of resignation, not accusation. Looking up at her face,
I added a tinge of coercion to that tone. She hoped she could wear
me down through careful applications of guilt and concern. A
long time ago, Irene Adler was a lauded soprano, only catching
the eye of Sherlock Holmes when one of her paramours, a king
no less, convinced the great detective to steal an important photo
from her. She had outwitted Holmes and applied her skills to the
wrong side of the law — half to dare him to catch her and half out

of boredom. After fifty years of dodging and catching Sherlock Holmes, the woman was a formidable foe. One that I didn't intend to get on the wrong side of — grandmother or not.

I shook my head at her, pointing to an earlier answer I had given on my pad of paper, "I'm fine."

I had passionately petitioned for my release from the hospital as soon as my burns had healed beyond Watson's care. I was still taking a veritable cocktail of pills three times a day, but even agreeing to that had seemed like heaven compared to being trapped in a hospital room where friends, family, and the occasional squadron of medical students paraded through to point at the freak who spoke in tongues. So adamant was the good doctor about my pill regimen that he assigned a nurse to drop off my medication once a week at my home on Baker Street. I only agreed with the caveat that Brian's medication for his burns be dropped off at the same time.

Unfortunately, two days in my own home had turned out to be only slightly better. My grandmother refused to leave my side. Here from morning until she tucked me in at night, and when she went out for even an hour, Annie showed up, or Brian, or his mother, Mrs. Dawes. At least the Dawes were my tenants at Baker Street, living in the downstairs apartment, but Annie had to haul herself in from Spital Street to check up on me and she was too busy for that nonsense. She was writing a story about the ladies-in-waiting who found themselves defending the queen and her king against the common people. The Mistress of the Robes, Ms. Wilans, was the older woman in the newspaper photo who had captured my eye, and according to Annie, she was not the approachable type. Fortunately for my reporter friend, the younger ladies had much to say about the limitations they felt in this new publicly hostile environment.

Even with the distraction of possibly living the rest of my life without sound or speech, it was day two of my being stuck under my grandmother's watchful eye and I really couldn't take much more of it.

Nerissa was the only one enjoying my house arrest. The bloodhound snuggled at my feet or pressed her soft, velvety head against my hand until I obligingly petted her.

I wrote the following to my grandmother, "I am going to the Yard before lunch. Then to the college for what I've missed, and then home to Nerissa, and ONLY Nerissa. I love you, but I will go mad if forced to live like a watched zoo animal for much longer."

I gave the older woman a hug before I handed the note to her, hoping she wouldn't be too hurt by me essentially throwing her out of my home.

She read and then looked up at me, so I squeezed her hand for emphasis. She fetched a deep sigh, taking the notebook from me to write, "Shocked it took this long for you to lose patience. Fine. I need to research better doctors and this revolving door of nurses who show up with your pills is unacceptable. Promise you will rest?"

I read this note, rolling my eyes, but nodding at her affectionately and helping her get dressed to leave.

I closed the door behind my grandmother and said to my bloodhound, "Well, that could have gone much worse."

Nerissa's tongue lolled out of her mouth. A perfect response.

CHAPTER 5

WITHIN A HALF HOUR of gaining my freedom from my loving grandmother, I left my Baker Street apartment for Scotland Yard. I had written a note for the motor cab driver before I walked out my front door and handed it to him as I entered his vehicle. The note simply said, "I cannot hear or speak. Please take me to the back entrance of Scotland Yard. Write the fare on this note and pass it back to me when we arrive."

Despite my instructions, the man continued to talk during the drive, either not believing me or forgetting every few blocks. I listened intently to his drumming rhythmic voice, but could not distinguish any words.

I got out of the cab into the crisp cold air outside the Yard, waving the cabbie away and slowly making my way up the stairs. I passed people, who were smoking and milling about as usual, but the silence was absolute in my head, except for some dull drumming that signalled conversations.

Several officers stopped me as I made my way around desks and chairs, and I was forced to tell my tale again and again using my notebook. Their sympathetic looks felt like spiders creeping over my skin, so I quickly made my way to Inspector Michaels' door, refusing to make any more eye contact along the way.

I raised my hand to knock and then realized I would not hear any answer if one should be made. I knocked anyway and waited, my ear pressed against the windowed part of the door.

I jumped at the tap on my shoulder, of course not having heard anyone approach me. My partner, Brian, stood there, his eyes anxious as he put a hand on my shoulder and said something I could not understand. I couldn't help but notice that the purple splotches under his eyes persisted and he looked very tired.

I shook my head, feeling all eyes in the room on us and hating the pity I could almost taste flowing in my direction and it tasted bitter indeed.

I put my hands over my ears in a quick gesture to remind him of my deficiencies.

He nodded, taking the notepad from my hands and leading me to his desk to take a seat.

"We should keep trying, shouldn't we?" he wrote.

It wasn't like I was going to fail to spot an improvement in my hearing, I thought with simmering anger. Writing, "There's no need to test me every time you see me."

He read my words and then looked up at me, his face apologetic.

I snatched the notepad from his surprised grip to write, "Stop looking at me like I'm damaged."

I pushed the notepad back at him and folded my arms over my chest. He picked up the pen, his hand hesitant over the page for a second before he wrote, "You have the right to be angry, but I didn't cause the explosion."

I looked from the words he had written to his left hand, still bandaged up and stiff, wondering again at his unspoken pain. Especially compared to my loud complaints.

I picked up the pen. "I came looking for my camera and Michaels."

"Your camera is in evidence and probably beyond repair. Michaels is upstairs interviewing new prospective sergeants."

So, his promotion came through, I thought to myself, nodding to Brian, and automatically thanking him aloud. He frowned, making me wonder what I had said instead of what I meant to say.

"How is the case progressing? Have you pursued any leads with the IRA?" I wrote. The bomb would be an odd choice for the Irish Republican Army, but the targets might be right for their agenda. "I told you about the protestors, right? The ones from the Irish Feminist League?"

Two constables passed by Brian's desk as he wrote an answer and I noticed that the younger of the pair had been recently digging by the condition of his knees and the dirt under his fingernails. Seemed a little odd for this time of year, my eyes travelling up his person to his lips, which were actively in conversation with his peer. I stared at his mouth, trying to understand when Brian tapped me again, this time on my hand.

He raised both his hands at me, forgetting his injuries for a second, shuddered at the painful reminder, and slid his injured hand behind his back. He took a deep steadying breath before writing, "The bomb is all wrong for the IRA. I'll grab the case file for you."

Suddenly, a chief inspector wearing suspenders ran out of one of the side offices and the twenty-odd men in the room snapped to attention. I watched as the chief inspector pointed at several of the men. They went off scurrying in one direction and another bunch ran off in another direction. I had started to write a note to Brian so that I could find the source of the excitement, but he was already engaged with another group of constables, all looking very serious. None of them paid me any attention and sprang off on different courses, leaving me basically alone in the middle of the empty bullpen with no idea what was going on.

I closed my eyes, wearily rubbing the bridge of my nose. When I opened them, it was to write a note to Brian asking him to bring the case file home with him to Baker Street. I left the note on his desk and dragged myself out of the deserted station.

Even my journey from the Yard to King's College was exasperating. I ran into Ruby, a homeless child who was one of my Baker Street Irregulars — the network of Londoners I sometimes paid to do my street-level reconnaissance. I found Ruby and her little band of children to be especially effective because they had access to the underbelly of the city and were the sadly anonymous class of citizens who were neither noticed nor remembered.

Unfortunately, the access Ruby and her peers had to London did not include access to the school system. She couldn't read the piece of paper I handed her and she certainly couldn't write whatever she was trying to convey to me down.

Finally, after five minutes of fruitless attempts at communication, I grabbed her dirty hands from waving around as she repeated her narrative for the third time. The two girls who were with her scampered out of my reach and Ruby jumped at my touch, her eyes narrowing suspiciously. I relaxed my grip (well aware of the abuses these children suffered on the streets) and moved her hands so that they were over my ears. She still looked confused, so I shook my head with her hands still in place, and then moved her hands over my mouth, shaking my head again.

A small "O" of surprise formed on the young girl's mouth and she nodded slowly, starting to understand. I passed her a coin and a note, trying to communicate that she needed to find some-one to read it to her. She looked down at the note and shrugged, calling for her peers before walking away from me, looking over her shoulder every ten yards or so until she was out of my sight.

I continued my walk to King's College, trying not to make eye contact with anyone, but noticing a woman on her way to work who had left her front door open as evidenced by the way she was carrying her keys, with her house key still out and pointed in front of her. I waved her down, but she was in too much of a hurry to wait and said something incomprehensible to me before running off to her seamstress job.

By the time I had arrived at my destination, I was in no mood for dealing with the public. I had my hand on the door leading into the building where I had spent the last three years working towards my law degree when a herd of people rushed past me to get outside. I was buffeted about by all the moving bodies, but somehow managed to get inside, pressing myself against the hallway wall.

People continued their frenzied exit, some without their winter coats, gathering in a space off the school grounds across the street. I recognized a few of the women in my third-year class and even saw one call to me, her eyes meeting mine as she drew close. When I didn't respond, she grasped my arm and tried to pull me out the door I had just come in. I shook off her hand and went in the opposite direction, looking for the source of the panic.

That was when my friend Beans came around the corner. The awkward son of Lord Beanstine and professor at King's saw me, registered surprise on his handsome bespectacled face. The drum beats of his speech got louder as he approached my position. He ignored my attempts to communicate and grabbing my waist nearly lifted me off my feet to get me out of the building.

I gave up protesting as soon as we were outside, but he seemed not to notice, continuing his rapid departure until we were across the street from the college and well into the small park. Only there was I able to convince him to release me as he encouraged other students and faculty to join us where we stood, waving his arms. For all of Lord Beanstine's very vocal contempt for his son's chosen profession, Henry Beanstine demonstrated his leadership in ways his father would never appreciate. Suddenly, I felt a rumble under my feet and everyone in the crowd seemed to surge in a singular direction. A plume of smoke rose from a building to the east, far from where we were gathered, but close enough that all around me students cowered on the grass, helping each other up from prostrate positions. I thought I was the only one still standing tall, the sound of the explosion much less dramatic to my ears, and not having reacted instinctively by throwing myself out of harm's way.

Except I wasn't.

A young girl on crutches a hundred yards away stood staring at me, equally unique in the sea of humans frantically scurrying around us. She seemed unfazed by the panic around her and singular in her reaction. I cut through the crowd, pushing people out of my way, her eyes — one hazel, one green — standing out in her small white face, burned into my psyche.

"Hey!" I called out, not caring what I actually said, only hoping to slow her down, but she joined the natural currents of the throng, throwing aside her crutches, weaving out of my sight within moments.

CHAPTER 6

"THREE BOMB THREATS IN the same afternoon?" I wrote on my pad of paper, sitting next to Brian at dinner that same night.

I could feel a very faint vibration coming from the other end of the table we sat at and, glancing up, was unsurprised to see Mr. Dawes with his chin on his chest, his belly passing his snores into the table.

In the meantime, Brian put down his fork to hold up five fingers before writing, "Buckingham Palace — where I was deployed. That one was mailed to the Yard. Other four were called in. Only real bomb was at Grey Hall and no one was hurt."

His bandaged left hand was now covered in a black glove and though he had taken four pills at the beginning of the meal, I could tell that the pain persisted an hour later. He was fidgeting with his pill bottle and glancing at the clock every quarter of the hour.

"Those are targets the IRA would find useful to threaten."

We exchanged a look as I wrote those words before Brian pressed pencil to paper again to answer.

"Michaels believes it is more likely to be Russians. Holdovers from the war that have been reactivated by Moscow."

"Was there a warning before the bomb at the railway station?" I wrote as Mrs. Dawes picked up our plates. The sting of Brian and his peers tearing off to Buckingham Palace was still very present … it was the ease with which I was dismissed as irrelevant at Scotland Yard that continued to smart. Even the fact that I had been present at the explosion on the college campus seemed irrelevant to the police. They didn't even bother to interview me as a witness.

Brian snagged a final carrot off his plate before she could leave, earning an indulgent smile from his mother.

I tapped the pad a little impatiently as they spoke, drawing his attention back to me.

He flipped open the case file to point to the rail engineer's statement.

He glanced suddenly away from me and held up a finger. Another second went by and he rose, leaving the table to exit his front door into our shared hallway. I surmised that someone had rung the bell to 221 Baker Street and my suspicion was confirmed when he strode back in with Dr. Heather Olsen a few moments later.

Dr. Olsen was a practicing psychiatrist and my half-cousin, her father and my mother were step-siblings, two of Dr. John Watson's children by different mothers. Olsen's father was the outcast of the Watson clan and he had removed himself and his small family from his father's and his brothers' lives. Olsen was her name by marriage of course. She had married someone too much like her own father and left him soon after.

She smiled at me before being introduced by Brian to his mother. I let their conversation continue for a few moments — time seemed to pass so much slower when silence enveloped it — before tapping on my pad to indicate to Olsen that she needed to use it to communicate with me.

She surprised me by handing me a note she had already written that said, "I came to check up on you and introduce you to a friend who might be able to help."

I looked up at her questioningly, but followed her back out into the hallway where a woman a little younger than me stood waiting, her brown colouring a gorgeous contrast to her pale dress. Originally from France, if her footwear was any indication, she raised her hand in greeting when she saw me and made a few gestures. To my surprise, Olsen responded with more hand gestures.

I watched their hand conversation with curiosity until Olsen tapped on the note she had handed me, and I flipped it over, "This is Amélie from the Institut National de Jeunes Sourds in Paris. She's going to teach you to read lips."

CHAPTER 7

I DIDN'T WANT TO like Amélie because I had zero interest in learning to read lips, but her unshakeable smile made it hard to follow through on my plans.

The small woman had twisted her long, black braids into a scarf that matched her dress and smelled incredible, like jasmine and honey. To my chagrin, I had to ask after her perfume. She laughed and wrote down the name of it under my question, "Shalimar."

Heather explained to me over tea and my pad of paper that in consultation with the doctors Watson, they had contacted the French school for the deaf and were put into contact with one of their most accomplished graduates — Mademoiselle Amélie Blaise, who was living in London. She and Dr. Olsen had met and Amélie had offered to work with me.

I tried to be polite through these drawn-out explanations — they took forever because of the amount of reading and writing they required — but explicitly refused the offered aid.

$$\backsim$$

"EVERYONE GOES THROUGH WHAT you are going though when they lose one of their abilities; soldiers who have lost a limb, an elderly person who loses their sight," said the note written by Olsen.

I gritted my teeth and wrote back, "That information does nothing to help me, Doc. I resent being condescended to or pitied."

What I didn't write was that my abilities were what made me distinct. What was I without my inductive skills? Just another immigrant Londoner from the colonies? An orphan with famous relatives? I fought the urge to glare at Amélie as she and Olsen talked back and forth with their hands.

Amélie pointed at a word on my notepad and demonstrated the sign. When I didn't respond, she did it again, adding a kind smile. I shook my head, but, almost against my will, mimicked her sign, following along as she went through some simple words. Then she asked Heather to say them out loud, one at a time, so that I could focus on how words were formed through the lips. Portia. Baker Street. Scotland Yard. But when she got to Brian, I shook my head again.

I wrote on my notepad, "I appreciate the help, but I would like you both to leave. I have much to do today and casebooks to review." I tried to pass it over, but to my surprise, found a note being passed to me first.

"You believe that because your abilities are superior, so too should the magnification of their loss," I read off her note, my eyes leaping to meet hers. I opened my mouth to deny it, remembered why I was writing notes instead, and angrily blinked away my tears.

Olsen reached out to cover my hand with hers and, looking straight at me, blew out all her breath. When I looked confused, she did it again and then raised her eyebrows at me.

I finally understood and after taking a moment to dramatically roll my eyes, I blew all the breath out of my body, calming my racing heart.

"You have emotional and mental issues to overcome too. I can help," she wrote.

She wrote on the notebook and then spoke to me as the other woman signed the words one at a time.

"Remember when you first got here? It was so hard to be taken seriously as a detective. You overcame."

I glanced over at Amélie, who was nodding and signing something at the doctor.

"Amélie says you will surprise them again," she wrote, smiling at her young friend as she passed the notebook back to me. Could I do it again? Fight through the derisive drumbeat against my gender, my outsider-status as a Canadian, and worst of all, the old-boys club of detective work? I must have transmitted these feelings on my face because Heather picked up the pencil again.

"Don't tell me you're scared of the fight," she wrote.

I blew my breath out again in response, rising to get my afternoon medication as the two women laughed at my reaction. I did not share their ease.

CHAPTER 8

SEVERAL DAYS LATER I sat in my usual café, having my usual Saturday breakfast, trying to hear the people around me. Normally, I picked a table in a corner so as to enjoy my meal in quiet, but today I handed a note to my waiter asking for a central location. He looked puzzled, but did as I asked. I sat warming my hands as they wrapped around my tea and looked from table to table, straining to hear actual words rather than underwater sounds of conversation.

The smells in the room were sharper to me today: the sweetness of the cake tray as it passed my seat, and the pungent carafes of coffee that sat on the tables around me. I noticed that my perfume had faded to the point that I could not detect it anymore and reminded myself to look into Amélie's distracting perfume. My grandmother was constantly trying to introduce me to new beauty products; it might be time to allow for that.

Among the few bright spots were my evening visits with Brian, which I had missed while trapped at the hospital. Last night I noted that he smelled of clean soap and peppermint as usual, but with an underlying scent all his own. It was the first time I had ever noticed that. We were both hesitant of each other's injuries, carefully avoiding bruises and burns, but at least we were alone again. He was less receptive to my report on the young girl who had seemed unfazed by a bomb blast that had dropped everyone else to the ground. I didn't know how the girl was involved. She might not be, but her reaction was unexplainable and that made it important, to me at least.

His reaction made me think of the last thing Olsen had written to me before leaving my rooms. She asked how Brian was recovering from his injuries and, while I knew her to be far more empathetic than I, I wondered why she was asking. She had hesitated before answering, eventually writing that people handle pain in different ways and that Brian's personality and pressures might make him unwilling to deal with his trauma, putting them aside because he was the head of his family. At the very least, she suggested I watch for uncharacteristic reactions and his dismissive response to the girl could be considered uncharacteristic. He was usually flatteringly interested in my views.

A tap on my shoulder brought me out of my solitary thoughts. My waiter said something incomprehensible to me and then pointed out the window, where I could clearly see Ruby and two of her small peers standing outside the café. I had sent another note with another of her peers after the bombing, asking for her help identifying the girl at the college bombing. She must have found something. Whatever the waiter was saying, their appearance was clearly upsetting him, so I wrapped up my untouched pastry in a napkin, put a few coins on the table, and left without trying to communicate any further. By now, Londoners should be more sympathetic to their fellow human beings left out in the cold while fewer and fewer of us actually had the means to enjoy a meal in a restaurant. But there was no point in trying to explain that to this man, I thought to myself, pushing the glass door open to the cold morning air.

Ruby waved at me, and then elbowed one of the boys who had

accompanied her, who handed me a dirty piece of newsprint upon which he had written the words, "No sine of girl wit cruches."

I wasn't surprised. The only details I had been able to pass on were a rudimentary description of her face and height — a near impossible assignment even for industrious scouts like these. Spying the outdoor furniture for the café stacked in the alley, I led the children over to right a table and a few chairs so that we might sit in the relative protection provided by the two buildings.

Handing the pastry to Ruby, I pulled out my own notebook to write a response while she carefully divided the treat into three. I waited for the boy to scarf down his portion, and then handed him the notebook with my pencil. I had written one word with a drawing of a cross, hoping he would understand. The girl's crutches had been carefully wound with cloth and bunting, perhaps hinting that her condition was not a temporary one. That probably meant she frequented a doctor's office or hospital for ongoing care.

He looked down at it, scratched his head, and then answered a question from Ruby, who was looking down at the note curiously. She nodded and said something back to him, which he leaned over the table to carefully write, holding my pencil uncertainly over the paper in his hand.

"Arnie an his crew werk Harley street," his note answered. "We can chek wit dem."

"Please tell Arnie there is more where this came from for all of you," I wrote, handing the note to the boy and handing a coin to Ruby.

CHAPTER 9

LATER THAT SAME DAY I sat waiting impatiently for Inspector Michaels to reappear at his desk. Twice I waved away concerned officers, and twice I stood up, walked around, and then immediately sat back down when I realized my impatience made the office stare at me anew.

Finally, Michaels came into view as he clomped down the stairs across the room from where I sat waiting. I assumed the clomping sound because I was used to hearing it when he walked those stairs, the distinctive sound of his walk known to me at this point. I stood up again and quickly made my way towards him as he sent one of his detectives off in one direction and signed something on a clipboard for another.

He noticed me and actually gave a small smile in my direction, saying something that I could not hear. I shook my head to confirm that I still hadn't regained my hearing and his smile faded, to be replaced with the dreaded response of pity as he waved me into his office. I shook off my negative reaction to his concern and followed him in, noticing the hint of perfume hovering on his uniform. Unless I was mistaken, his relationship with my cousin Heather had progressed. That was her perfume — an older Chanel bottle that had been watered down, something I had remarked on a few months ago and she had admitted to having bought off the back of a truck. Welcome to London in an economic downturn.

I pulled out my notebook as he manoeuvred himself behind his desk, taking out a cigar and lighting it before taking the note I extended his way.

"I may have a lead, but I need your help to investigate," was what the note said, and it got its planned reaction from the large man as he yanked out his cigar to demand, "Who?"

I still couldn't hear him, but I mentally catalogued the shape of his lips before I could stop myself and tapped the note I had handed him. He impatiently flipped it over to read the rest, "A young girl I saw at the college before the bomb exploded."

"Girl?" he barked at me and again I was able to read his lips based on what I anticipated his questions would be. He realized that he was speaking and how fruitless that was, so with a shake of his head, he flipped open his own notebook on his desk and scratched out a few sentences while flakes of cigar ash fell over his work. Brushing those off, he handed the note to me and then swung his attention towards his door.

I took the note to read, "Unless this little girl was carrying a batch of mines in her handbag, I'm more concerned about your partner. He's been late three times this week."

Brian was never late, but even if he were, I was not his keeper. I needed the Yard's constables to find this girl. In my current state I was half the investigator I usually was. I turned to see Michaels in conversation with one of his men and then he ran back behind his desk, collecting his overcoat. He looked at my note asking for help and, to my growing anger, waved it away, pointing at me and then at the officer in the doorway and barking orders at both of us.

He practically bolted out of his office and I made to follow him but was stopped physically by the officer, a man I had never met. He tried to make hand gestures to make me understand what he was saying, but I pushed him aside to follow Inspector Michaels out of Scotland Yard and into the police car he had just stopped outside the building.

I clambered inside the backseat of the car, ignoring Michaels' protests, which I couldn't hear, but could most certainly deduce from his angry mouth and pointing finger. I stoically sat next to him, facing forward with my arms crossed over my chest. He very quickly figured out that I was not getting out of the car and it started moving on his order.

Once we got moving, I passed my notebook over to Michaels. I had written, "If you won't help, then at least tell me where we are going."

He looked down at the paper and then rolled down the window to tap his cigar before replacing it in his mouth and taking up my pencil to answer.

"There's been another threat. Downing Street," he wrote back hurriedly.

I felt a little jolt at reading that note; Downing Street was, after all, the main office of the British government, and I quickly wrote, "The prime minister? The cabinet?"

Michaels read the note as we pulled up — Downing Street being under half a mile from Scotland Yard — and shook his head as we exited the vehicle, frustrating me to no end as that could mean anything.

I hesitated as I closed the car door behind me. Outside the political offices of the British Government, police had set up a cordon that reminded me very much of the scene where Constable Bonhomme had lost his life and I had lost everything else.

Michaels seemed to sense that hesitation in me so I forced

myself to nod at him, following his lead as he stepped up to speak to one of the officers to let us through the cordon. The building had obviously been evacuated, as evidenced by the number of secretaries and clerks standing out in the cold without their coats. If any of the upper echelon of the government had been here, they would have been taken somewhere safe, off-site and away from the growing crowd of curious Londoners.

I looked around at the melee and sighted Brian directing a few officers as they came out of the front door of 10 Downing Street. Quickly I made my way to his side, tapping him on the shoulder when I got close enough. He turned and immediately frowned, shaking his head when I tried to hand him my notebook.

If I had been just a little younger, and a little less mature, I would have thrown a fit at the dismissal I was receiving today, but as such, I just stepped around Brian and into 10 Downing Street through the open door. No one stopped me, at least physically. I wouldn't be able to tell if they tried to stop me with words, so I headed up the stairs, nodding at officers I recognized as I made a visual perimeter of the place. It was a bit of a thrill to be within these walls, both for me and I could tell for a few of the younger officers who were inside the building for the first time. I took in everything from the rugs to the wooden details to the number of steps and the wear on the treads even as I noted that a constable had been posted outside each door as the inside of the room was searched by another.

Most of the police activity seemed to be concentrated on the first floor, so I made my way up to the second and then the third.

Only one door in the hallway seemed to be both unmanned and unsearched, and that attracted my eye. Unlike the others it had neither a room number nor a window into its interior. It could have been a cupboard, though its location seemed less than optimal up here on the third floor, which served as a private residence rather than offices. I sniffed at the door, but couldn't detect the smell of cleaning supplies that you would expect in a spot where you store mops and buckets, nor the clean laundry smell of a linen closet. I smelled cigarettes, but no sooner had I reached for the doorknob than a long-fingered brown hand covered mine, making me jump. I had not heard anyone try to speak to me nor had I sensed someone that close. I turned, my eyes meeting a pair of dark brown ones, belonging to a man a little older than me, his face as handsome as I had ever encountered, with a cleft chin and high cheekbones. He was the source of the cigarette smell.

He spoke then, though so softly that the usual drumming wasn't detectable for my injured ears. His breath smelled of bubble gum, which surprised me, as I took in his naval uniform, glancing at his hands and the waves of his hair and deciding that he was not what he seemed. Commanders of African descent were still quite rare in the Royal Navy. He repeated whatever he had tried to say the first time, an encouraging smile on his lips, so I took my hand off the doorknob to reach into my bag for my notebook.

With a speed I had not seen before, he crushed me against the wall, a slim knife appearing out of nowhere and now pressed against my throat.

I dared not scream, though I was relatively sure that I could communicate terror despite my communication issues, and instead stared right back at him defiantly. The fact that I chose not to struggle or scream seemed to confuse the man and I felt his grip on me loosen, though his body still held me in place so that I could feel every muscle pressed against me. He spoke again, this time directly into my ear. I still couldn't hear a thing, but I

THE DETECTIVE AND THE SPY   41

guessed that he wanted to know who I was as much as I wanted
to know who he was.

I managed to pull the note I had used in the cab out of my
pocket and I slowly slid it between our bodies to show him. He
quickly scanned the note and only then did he lower the knife,
though I still couldn't take a deep breath while I was flattened
into the wall by his body. His eyes ran over the fading bruises
on my face as I slowly placed my hands over my mouth, shook
my head, and then placed them over my ears and shook my head
again. When he still looked suspicious, I tapped the note in his
hand and mimed writing.

He finally seemed to understand what I was trying to say and
I felt his body's heat recede, allowing me to stand on my own
two feet again. Glancing down the hallway to see if we were still
alone, he slid the knife into his pocket. That was when I gripped
his belt with both hands, slammed my knee into his groin, and
shoved him as hard as I could away from me.

He went down like a stone, completely silent as far as I could
tell. I didn't stop to see if he got back up, but sprinted away from
him and down the stairs as quickly as I could. I got to the main
floor where Brian and two officers stood conversing in low
drumming tones with another man dressed in a Navy uniform.
Seeing my distress, Brian pulled me to him and when I pointed
up the stairs, ordered his men to investigate, following them
up the stairs a little shakily. The man he had been speaking to
was an ensign I didn't know and I ignored him when he tried to
speak to me. Brian came back down, sweat beading his forehead,
and motioned his arms with palms upward to explain that no
one had been found. He spoke to the ensign, who agreed with
whatever Brian was saying, and everyone ignored my attempts
to show them the spot where I had been attacked. I pulled the

ensign up the stairs where he opened the closet door and waved his hands around inside, as if to prove to me that it was just a broom closet.

I restrained myself from shoving him into said closet in response, but Brian seemed to take whatever he was saying at face value, taking my elbow with a grim look. I didn't argue as he escorted me from the building, but as soon as we were outside I yanked my elbow away, disgusted at being once again dismissed like a child. Instead, I scanned the throng of people outside the building for the face of the man who had attacked me. Brian was trying to get my attention, walking in front of me, and then again when I purposefully turned away. He gave up then, angry, and stalked away. I had a brief instinct to reach out and stop him, but instead my eyes stuck on a group of secretaries being led away from the building. There was something about one of the women that reminded me of the young girl on the crutches.

I followed the officer and the women he was escorting, getting as close as I dared to the woman who displayed the same heterochromia that I had seen that day in the crowd — one eye hazel, the other green. Purposely, I bumped the arm holding her handbag by its fingerloop, so that it dropped to the cobbled road between us.

"Sorry," I mumbled as I stooped to help her pick up the items that had spilled out, a tube of lipstick, an invoice for a language class, a letter addressed to a Maj. Collins, a limp coin purse and half packet of biscuits.

Her face was a combination of annoyance and confusion, but I took a careful look at her hands as she picked up her items and placed them carefully in their proper spots in her purse, around an item wrapped in a stained kerchief. I sniffed the air and caught the faint scent of gun oil, perhaps indicating what was wrapped in the kerchief. She leaned away from me, suspicious for good reason, and walked away to rejoin her colleagues, glancing over her shoulder, perhaps to be sure I wasn't following. Though it was unusual for women to carry guns, it was not unheard of in this economic climate when brazen daylight thefts were on the rise. Nothing here directly linked her to the girl I had seen in that crowd except for their remarkable eyes and the wariness with which they regarded me.

CHAPTER 10

I PUT DOWN MY library book on genetics and hereditary traits to scribble down some data. Of course, there were more than two women in London with heterochromia, but there were other facial similarities. Enough for me to suspect the women were related. Similar eye size in relation to the size of their faces, attached earlobes, and a shared widow's peak. I had my mother's eyes and according to photos of my father, shared his wavy dark hair, which he in turn had inherited from his own mother, Irene Adler. I had spent three hours going through photos of students at the college, but had not found the face of the girl on the crutches in any of them. Of course, she could be shy, or not involved in extra-curricular activities, and to be honest, she seemed young for college classes. Two women who might be related at two different crime scenes? Coincidence or just one of London's big-city-small-world quirks?

Over on the wall next to the door I had a large map of London, a useful relic from when Holmes and Watson had lived in this apartment. It included codes and a notebook corresponding to the codes, detailing hidden aspects of alleyways and buildings that were fronts for criminal activities in the 1890s when he and Watson had been active. In my work, I added pins when I had a current case, keeping my own coded notebook of explanation, and right now, the pins were placed wherever a bomb threat had been reported. Where a bomb had actually exploded, I wound a yellow string around it. The pins weren't in a cluster, but I had included pins (wound in blue thread) for the call boxes closest to the targets. Staring at this map, I thought about places where you could call in a bomb threat and then watch from a safe distance as the mayhem ensued. I walked up to the pin at the train station. There were only two call boxes within viewing distance, but there were three pubs. I would have to check them out.

I looked at all the tomes on the table, noticing that some of them were not mine. Heather and Amélie had been busy. Amélie had been over to my apartment twice more to try and help me learn basic sign language, but when I went downstairs to Brian's apartment to get him to help with the lip-reading the way Annie had, I was told by his mother that he hadn't come home yet. There were four books on sign language and lip-reading. I reached out a hand to open one and then pulled it away like the books were an open flame. I wouldn't need them and I wouldn't need any more of Amélie's help. I was going to recover from this affliction. To open those books was to admit that this could be a permanent state. And that was unthinkable.

The second unfortunate discovery was that Nerissa had been locked in my bedroom and I hadn't heard her desperate attempts to communicate her need to be taken for a walk. She had expressed her need on the rug near the foot of my bed. With a sigh, I quickly bundled up the rug, my nose wrinkled against the smell, and threw it into my bathtub with some soap and water to let it soak.

I could scarcely be angry at my bloodhound; she had probably been trying to get my attention since I walked in the door. I apologized to her with a hug, and leashed her, deciding we could both use the walk.

It was bitingly cold tonight, so the park was all but deserted except for a homeless man on a bench, who, according to the movement of his mouth, was having a long conversation with the birds gathered around him. Nerissa ran off into the gorse bushes as usual and the squirrels she surprised came pelting out the other side, no doubt challenging her with their high-pitched chirps, which I remembered but could not hear.

I had to go back to the beginning — to the motive. Why was someone warning the police and then carrying out bombings that neither killed people nor allowed for other crimes like theft? What was the motive? Terrorism was usually linked to some group to make a point. Was there a bigger plan or was this bomber just an amateur? Was the girl at the college also suffering from a disability such as mine? Is that why she hadn't reacted? And who was the man with the slim knife? I needed more data and my usual skills were not up to the task.

I sat down on a bench, my mind returning to the man who had attacked me as the smell of bubble gum and Morlands wafted over the breeze and I realized with a shock that it was not just a memory. I whirled to look at the bench where the homeless man had been sitting and cursed aloud.

I called Nerissa to my side and strode to the bench he had so recently occupied, looking down the park lanes in both directions. He was long gone. I slumped my way home feeling discouraged, but it wasn't until later that night when I was swallowing my handful of pills that I realized that Nerissa had come when I called. Maybe I had managed to say her name?

I ran down the stairs at top speed, knocking on the apartment door to 221A. I had to knock three times before the door was opened and almost before he had fully opened the door, I said, "Brian."

He rubbed at his eyes, and said something, maybe "yes?" in answer, obviously I had woken him from a deep sleep.

I grasped his arm and said it again, "Brian."

He finally understood and gave a whoop, his eyes going wide. I grinned from ear to ear as he started babbling at me, still not hearing any of his words.

I shook my head and when he wouldn't stop talking at me, grasped him by the sides of his face and kissed him solidly on the mouth.

When I stepped back he was still grinning like an idiot which made me realize that we were both in our bedclothes. I stepped back, blushing, and said, "Tomorrow."

He seemed to understand because he nodded and said it back to me, "Tomorrow." He waited for me to climb my stairs before he closed his front door.

CHAPTER 11

BUT SUNDAY WAS A step backwards in every way. Though Brian and I tried for a half hour on my couch, my words were once again jumbled and wrong. It put a damper on our ardour because instead of enjoying Brian's lips, I found myself carefully watching his mouth and trying to interpret his whispered questions, only getting about one in ten words right. Trying to communicate what we wanted, what felt good, became guesswork. So much so that I pushed him away, his flushed face and half-closed eyes turned questioning and then disappointed. He left without an argument (or at least one I could participate in), carefully picking his shirt off the floor with his right hand on the way out, his left still bandaged. I let my blood cool for a few minutes and then, against my instincts, opened the book Heather had left behind on lip-reading and read it cover to cover. I hated the drawn images and I hated the advice and most of all I hated that I had been reduced to this condition. And then of course I felt the guilt over spending twenty-four years of my life with all my senses when people like Amélie lived happier lives with less. But her livelihood didn't depend on deduction.

I tried standing in front of the mirror to practise reading my own lips, but since I wasn't sure I was saying the words I intended to say, that exercise just left me angry at my body's betrayal.

In addition, two clients who had hired me to help with their cases had sent notes absolving me of my detective assignments. They were notes full of sympathy, quoting the injuries reported by various newspapers, but I absorbed each word like it was a carefully embedded splinter, dully painful and living beneath my skin. My skills were diminished and so too was my value to society. Even my value as a companion to the man I had fallen in love with seemed damaged. His pain was constant and not limited to his hand. Writing back and forth I wasn't able to coerce the level of pain out of him, nor the treatment prescribed by the doctor. He didn't want to talk about it and he most certainly did not want to spend our time together writing about it.

Feeling epically discouraged, I decided to visit my grand-mother, hoping that she could cheer me up.

"The queen had better do something about all this bad publicity," she wrote in my notebook in the back of her Bentley, handing me a few newspapers she had folded to highlight the damning arti-cles. "She's coming off worse than the king for her spending and she doesn't have the benefit of a parliament to blame."

I shuffled papers featuring headlines that were bolder than usual in their attacks on the queen, noticing the stoic position-ing of Ms. Wilans again as she raised an umbrella against a pack of journalists stalking her charge. Forget the royal guard, this woman was the queen's most ferocious defender.

I held one of the newspapers up to the car window as we pulled up to our destination. Was that bandaging around Wilans' hands? What could a lady-in-waiting get into that would hurt both her hands like that? Was she actually beating the crowds away with her bare fists? It was hard to tell in this photo. I'd have to ask Annie if she could help me find the original.

"Good news," my grandmother wrote in my notebook as we

sat down in the lobby of the St. Ermin's Hotel while being served tea and fresh strawberry scones. "There is a clinic in Switzerland that specializes in brain trauma cases. I have secured you a room there starting in June."

I tried to convey a sense of gratitude, but failed miserably. The idea of suffering under these conditions any longer was stifling and a clinic in Switzerland sounded unbearably depressing.

"But what about my work?" I wrote back to her. "And the college? I'm months away from graduating."

She assured me that the college would hold my place, or she'd make them hold exams that took my new disability into account, but that accommodation did not improve my mood. Who would hire a lawyer who couldn't even communicate? Or a consulting detective who couldn't speak to suspects or convince the police of their deductions?

As usual, she felt the best remedy for sadness was spending money, so we left the hotel for the shops, stopping often at windows so she could point out the latest fashions coming from Milan and Paris. She abjectly refused to come into the boutique armaments shop and after a few minutes sniffing expensive gun oils and annoying the staff, I left. As far as I knew, Holmes had done an exhaustive study of 140 tobaccos and their ash, but had never taken on gun oil. I decided I would be making my own monograph soon.

Thinking about smells, I was reminded of Amélie's scent and my grandmother was all too happy to take me to her favourite perfumery on Grosvenor Street to purchase two small bottles of Shalimar — one for me and one to thank Amélie. The dandy behind the counter was trying to sell my grandmother a small bottle of men's eau de toilette, but we both took a sniff and agreed it wasn't for any of the men in our lives. Too floral and spicy.

The tobacconist next door provided the confirmation I had

been looking for. I picked up a Balkan blend of Morlands, holding it to my nose and recognizing it immediately.

"For Brian?" asked my grandmother, a quirk on her lipstick-sheened lips.

I shook my head, paying for the cigarettes, my heart still sad about the way Brian and I had left things, but beating faster when I thought of the man with the knife.

I had decided not to tell my grandmother about the minor attack at Downing Street nor about my very brief recovery of my speech. The first would just upset her and the second would needlessly get her hopes up. My own hopes were exhausted, what with the promise of recovery and the regression of my symptoms. It was honestly tiring to be in a constant state of sensory flux.

I walked my grandmother back to her car where her driver was patiently waiting, turning down her offer to attend an upcoming ball, but promising to have dinner with her within the week. I decided to walk some of the way home — the day was cool after all, but the sun was shining, which was not always so in this city.

Standing on the platform at the tube, I looked from moving mouth to moving mouth, drawn to the lips, the responses, both vocalized and contained purely in the muscles of the face. Some of these Londoners were going to work, others coming home laden with shopping bags; all were able to communicate without even thinking about it, even with complete strangers. I glanced across the tracks and did a double take. Wasn't that Ms. Wilans herself? From here I could see her bandaged hands, an umbrella in one, an ancient alligator purse in the other, and that same crabby face I had come to recognize from the newspapers. I wasn't the only one who had recognized her. A group of young women were pointing and whispering in her direction and a man carrying one of the newspapers featuring her visage was looking from it to her and back again, his face betraying his growing anger. If these people couldn't find a queen to make pay for their financial troubles, her lady-in-waiting would do in a pinch. I was walking towards the tunnel that would take me to the north side of the tracks before any of them moved. Halfway down the tunnel I felt the rumble of the train pulling in above me and I broke into a run, sprinting up the stairs to the other side, onto the platform, and throwing myself through the train doors just in time. The train lurched into motion and I started looking for my lady-in-waiting. I moved from train car to train car, not seeing her, until Stepney Green, when out of the corner of my eye I caught her stepping off the train just as the doors closed.

I wasn't ready to give up. I got off at Mile End, impatiently waited for the train that would take me back, and then got off at Stepney Green less than ten minutes later. Obviously, Wilans was no longer in the station — why would she be — but I headed north, hoping that she might choose to stop at the market on her way home.

I passed several shops with Yiddish signs and a few Asian stores as well, the script flowing down and up and down again in beautiful columns meant to be read top to bottom and right to left. This was a part of London that was filled to the brim with immigrant culture, the sights and smells distinct and enticing, reminding me of my childhood in Cabbagetown. I shook my head at someone trying to sell me what looked like candied apples and smiled at a very serious couple pushing a baby carriage. They responded by doubling their speed and glancing back over their shoulders at me. The economic woes had hit this area hard and the number of children begging was almost double what you would find in the central parts of London. Their sad eyes looked up at me with a combination of hope and suspicion, so I stopped the man with the apples, bought ten of them and handed them out to the children in the alleyways between buildings. I remembered being this hungry. In Toronto, my mother had done her best to keep us clothed and fed, but there were more than a few mornings I went to school hungry, the breakfast money spent by my useless stepfather on booze the night before.

One older child, a Chinese boy, took the apple I gave him and immediately handed it to a smaller girl at his side, his eyes on me. He said something to me, so I took out my notebook and turned to the page that explained my situation. I handed it to him. To my surprise he read it and nodded, reaching out his hand for my pencil. I gave it to him and he wrote back in neat even handwriting, "We can help."

He beckoned me to follow him. I still hadn't seen hide nor hair of Wilans and my curiosity overrode my reservations as usual, so I followed him a block and a half and into a narrow herbal medicine shop.

The boy spoke to the woman behind the counter, their drumming sounds rhythmic and consistent, but different than any sounds I had heard before. I realized that they were probably not speaking English and almost smiled at the rhythmic differences that language added to conversation. The way the beats seemed to end on an upward lilt and sound like questions, even in the dulled way I heard conversation now. It was hard to explain, but I closed my eyes to concentrate on the sounds, cataloguing another clue I would never have picked up on before. Body language transcended race and language, these two were close, and trusted each other, their hand gestures very alike.

The boy mimed writing on my notepad. Bemused, I handed it to him, and he wrote, "My name is Lin. My aunt is a healer. Tell her what is wrong with you."

I wrote, "I was in an accident and I have a doctor. He says it will take time to heal."

"What kind of accident?" the boy wrote back after again exchanging words with his aunt.

I shook my head, writing, "Thank you, but I have all the help I need."

He read the note aloud to his aunt who pulled a scrapbook out from under the counter and flipped to a page and spoke to us again. I moved forward to see an article from *The Sunday Times* pasted onto the page, including a photo of myself in full consulting detective mode and a crowd of reporters behind me.

I looked to Lin and his aunt and tapped the image.

"You recognized me from this photo, Lin?" I wrote in my notebook.

He nodded on reading the note and on the encouragement of his aunt pointed to his earlier question, "What kind of accident?"

"An explosion. I was knocked backwards and my ears were damaged," I wrote back.

I could tell when the boy said the word explosion because the woman's eyes grew wide and she started speaking much faster, the staccato sound reminding me of rain hitting a pond, but deeper.

"And you cannot speak because of this?" the boy wrote, on the instruction of his grandmother.

I frowned, unsure how to answer this because no one seemed to know exactly why I couldn't speak, but before I could write an answer, the woman moved around the counter to reach up and grasp my face in her bronzed hands. The lady turned my face this way and that, pulled my left ear close, looked inside, and muttered under her breath, the smell of ginger floating off her as she chewed on a piece of the fresh vegetable.

Still holding my face, she motioned for me to speak, waving her hand at her throat and opening her mouth.

I said, "My name is Portia Adams and I live on Baker Street," waiting for and recognizing the look of confusion that came across the boy's face that confirmed that I was still speaking gibberish.

The aunt raised her chin and asked him something while I took back the pen to write an explanation, "I can say words, but the words I end up saying with my mouth are not the words I mean to say in my head."

She pulled at her nephew's sleeve and said something else to him that he wrote, "My aunt Chen asks if you are taking medicine for the accident."

I nodded, writing, "Three times a day, I take about fifteen pills. Why?"

"Do you have them with you?" he wrote directly underneath. I nodded, reaching into my satchel for a small pillbox and handing them to the older lady who had extended her hand for them. She shook a few out into her hand and then, carrying them to her counter, crushed one up in a mortar using a pestle. I wasn't really that concerned about the loss of one pill, but I tapped Lin's shoulder, shaking my head, hopefully indicating that I didn't want any more of my pills destroyed.

He shrugged, but said something to his aunt who, in the meantime, had added some oily liquid to the crushed pill and then, with her pinky finger, tasted the mixture, spitting it back out a second later.

"She says you must stop taking the medicine. That you are better already," Lin said.

I frowned as she pulled out a small canister and spoke to her nephew.

"Drink a cup of this tea every night instead of taking the medicine your doctor gave you. She says it will help your mind recover."

I had no intention of taking the advice of a woman I had just met over the Watsons, who had supervised my care since my accident, but I chose to write instead, "Why does she collect articles about me?"

Lin read the note and shook his head, not needing to ask his aunt before writing the answer. "It is not hers. The man who lived here before left it behind."

Curiouser and curiouser. I asked Lin if I could see the scrapbook and after a quick word with his aunt, he handed it to me. I flipped through it, finding to my surprise articles pasted in it that made no mention of me, but were cases I had been involved with behind the scenes. No other writing could be found on the pages, but I had an idea who this had belonged to. Someone who knew my methods intimately and had a mind that burned as brightly and unrelentingly as my own.

"The man who left this behind, was he a doctor?" I wrote to the young boy.

He nodded, so I asked, "Can I take this with me?"

He looked to his aunt who to my surprise shook her head, extending her hand for the scrapbook. I handed it back, not sure why she wanted to keep it, but unable to come up with another idea on how to convince her to give it to me.

"She says she keeps it as a ward against his return. She didn't like him," Lin had written in the meantime.

I didn't know if he would be back, but I wondered what Gavin had done to make this woman distrust him. I hoped for both our sakes that he would not return, because I did not relish the confrontation. I gave a small bow of thanks and left the small shop, my mind full of worries I hadn't walked in with.

CHAPTER 12

HE WATCHED HER LEAVE the small store alone, her uncharacteristically slow pace betraying her distraction. He knew that posture well. She had learned something from the shopkeeper and her nosy nephew. Portia Adams did not need a lot of data to start formulating a hypothesis. And he really didn't need her interference.

He leaned away, behind the ragged curtain as she looked around, eyes narrowed, another one of her habits. Constantly cataloguing. Constantly gathering information. Nothing escaped her gaze and once she had something between her teeth, she was a veritable bloodhound.

She finally seemed to come to a decision, walking back the way she had come.

She was adapting to her condition.

The part of him that loved her applauded her resilience. The part of him that was scared of her hated her for it.

CHAPTER 13

"SORRY PORTIA, MR. BENSON is taking his sweet time looking through his archives for mention of a Major Collins," the note Annie Coleson handed me read.

She then said aloud what she had written so I could practise recognizing the words on her lips, her finger hovering over each word as she said it the way Amélie had demonstrated.

She hadn't been able to help me much with Ms. Wilans either. None of the other ladies-in-waiting had mentioned an accident that could account for her injuries, but Annie promised to follow up with some of the more gossipy ladies and ask some discreet questions about the older woman.

I sighed, blowing out my breath so that my new bangs flew around my forehead. Annie had taken me to her favourite barber to finally fix the damage done to my hair. I had to admit, turning my head slightly so I could see the sides of my short cut in the mirror across from where I sat, the style suited me and would be far less work to maintain than the longer styles I had worn since I was a teenager in Toronto.

Annie grinned, seeing me looking at myself, and I stuck my tongue out at her. Annie had had short, curly blond hair since the day I had met her and nothing I ever did in a beauty salon would compete with her natural good looks. She was seeing

THE DETECTIVE AND THE SPY 59

someone new, but so far had not told me about him. I found it impossible to ignore the types of gifts he was lavishing upon her, the kind that spoke of wealth but anonymity. Gifts that would be hard to trace back to the giver. But I had learned from experience that it was best to allow my friends to tell me about new relationships rather than revealing that I had known about them for a long time.

I pulled the notebook back to me as she took another bite of her banana split, batting her eyelashes at the gentlemen who had just entered The Trifle café behind where I sat. This spot across from the War Office on Whitehall was frequented by officials of the government and their underlings because it was a block away from 10 Downing Street.

"So, what do really you think of Gavin's creepy scrapbook?" she wrote on the notepad.

I crossed out the word creepy and gave her a look.

She raised her hands in mock surrender but wrote, "Boyfriends aren't supposed to keep tabs on you. Ex-boyfriends even less so. So glad you broke up with that creep."

I bit my lip before I took the pencil she proffered, "He broke up with me. And you know that he was good to me before —"

She snatched the pencil before I could finish the sentence, "Oh no, Portia Adams," she said aloud, forgetting my issues.

I pulled another pencil out of my bag, "— before he decided that money and power were more important than me. Lesson learned, Annie. New subject?"

"I'm working on a story about stockpiling weapons," she admitted via the notepad. "Not my usual beat, but Henry Rees asked me to help him out. You know how he gets when he's chasing a rumour."

"Do you want to come with me to the War Office?" I wrote,

passing the notebook back to her and waving away her offered spoonful of ice cream.

She shook her head ruefully, writing, "No. I need to telegram my father in Sandwell. Haven't heard from him in weeks. Getting worried."

She passed the notebook back to me, giving a tiny wave to the men who now sat behind me. I sighed. Annie's secret relationship didn't keep her from flirting with anything in suspenders and a fine hat. One of the men took her up on her flirtation, strolling over to lean on the table and introduce himself to us. He extended a hand my way and I shook it dutifully before he dismissed me from his gaze to focus on my lovely friend, who smiled beatifically up at him. I turned away from the conversation I couldn't hear to lock eyes with the man who had held a knife to my neck at Downing Street. He blew a large pink bubble and before it had popped I had switched from my table to his, notebook in hand.

"Hello again," he said, if I'd read his lips correctly.

I wrote on my notepad, "Why are you following me?"

He said something I couldn't decipher from watching his mouth, so I tapped the notebook with my pencil. He gave a dramatic sigh that I could see if not hear, before reaching for the notepad and writing, "Who's following whom? You didn't show up at The Trifle just for the desserts, I'm sure."

Not being able to snap back a retort was so annoying, but worse, I was not at my best, and dealing with this man, I sensed I needed to be at my best. I slid the pack of Morlands I had bought for him with my grandmother and his smile wavered. He didn't like that I was creating a profile of him. I had landed a glancing blow. I had another.

"You're not a Navy man and you're not police," I wrote beneath his words. "You're with Box 850 aren't you?" The last time

I had had dealings with someone from Box 850, as the British Secret Intelligence Service was colloquially called, was with an unscrupulous agent who had turned from serving the British people to lining his pockets. I didn't know if the British Secret Intelligence Service employed many minorities in their spy ring, but I knew there were a few women in the service and I suspected this man would do well as a spy because no one would suspect him.

The man sitting in front of me leaned back his chair, that sexy smile that I'm sure other women found entirely disarming resurfacing as he opened his gift of cigarettes.

"Don't make me take another swing at the family jewels, you can't afford it," I wrote. "Who are you?"

I expected him to flinch at the memory, or at least glower, but this man was a strategist, plus a threat delivered by pencil and paper was not my most intimidating power. He pulled the paper back his way to write, "You can call me Lancaster. And don't worry, I'll never underestimate you again. By the way, what did you find out about Heddy Collins?"

Her name was Heddy Collins. What else did he know? I leaned over the table, intending to scrawl something incendiary, when I felt the lightest of vibrations through the table leg. I couldn't hear it because of my injuries, but was it normal that I should feel the vibration? Lancaster had leaned back again and I followed his eye line to two men sitting on barstools. He noticed me looking and continued his gaze as if he were enjoying the sight of a server leaning over a table, wiping it clean. I wasn't fooled. I recognized one of those men. If I wasn't mistaken, that was Éamon O'Duffy, of Sinn Féin ... and what *was* that vibration? I couldn't concentrate with that pattern knocking against my knee. I looked around for a large clock or a piano being played nearby. Nothing. I stood up, looking for the source of the rhythmic tremor, shutting everything else out, pressing my hand on the table to feel the consistent pulsation, barely discernible unless you really concentrated. I could hear the drumming of voices all around me, but they were easy to ignore, to push back into the silence that engulfed me. This was an entirely different sense, one that was not injured and it was fully engaged. I closed my eyes, running my hand down the table leg to the floor. It was slightly stronger here. It was pulsing from beneath the floorboards. I opened my eyes to meet the gaze of the man who wanted me to believe his name was Lancaster, his air of indifference long gone.

"What is it?" he asked me, enunciating slowly.

I tapped the floor with my hand. "Underneath us," I said.

He pressed his hand to the floor and then his ear to the floor for a few heartbeats, then leapt to his feet and spoke in a deep drumming voice. I didn't need to hear him to know he was telling people to leave the restaurant from the way they stood up and started gathering their things frantically. We both watched O'Duffy's reaction, but he just followed his friend out of the pub with a frown, his mouth moving constantly and unreadable through the crowd. Annie reached for me from her table, but her erstwhile beau (no doubt Lancaster's peer) picked her up in his arms and carried her out of the room. He was going to get an earful from her about his assumptions once he put her down. I got up from the floor and moved against the crowds, making my way to the kitchens. Behind the cooks and wait staff clamouring to leave I saw what I was looking for: stairs leading down.

I made my way down the dimly lit wooden stairs to a basement that was barely five feet high and obviously used for storage, refuse, and little else. The light switch was useless, so I pressed my hand to the ceiling of this basement and felt the multitude of vibrations of a room full of people leaving the building and then a second single vibration, the weighted footsteps of a man walking down the stairs to join me. Lancaster put his hand on my shoulder and I immediately picked it up and pressed it to the ceiling so that he might feel what I was feeling. That rhythm I had noticed had returned now that everyone had stopped moving. Crouching down, I moved forward, squinting in the darkness, already dreading what I was looking for. I turned to see him pointing at a small alarm clock attached to the ceiling of the basement with wires. We carefully pushed boxes of potatoes and onions out of the way, until we could crouch beneath it. The man pulled out a small torch and he pointed it up to reveal the face of the clock, the red alarm hand set to midnight and a wire leading out of it, also stapled to the ceiling. Following the wire with his torch light, I counted eleven bombs wired to eleven clocks, arranged in a circle that would surely destroy the main floor when detonated.

Lancaster pointed at the stairs adamantly. "Go. Now."

I shook my head, looking around for wire cutters amongst the boxes and shelves. If someone had placed this system of bombs and wiring down here surely they had used tools. Why had they used eleven clocks? Why not wire them all to one clock in sequence?

The man reached into his pocket to pull out the slim knife that had once been pressed against my throat in a hallway on Downing Street. He pointed it at the wires above us, and then at me, and then at the stairs.

"I'm not going anywhere," I muttered at him, not amused by his look of confusion at whatever word jumble had actually left my mouth.

I focused on the wires. Were they armed to trip if we were to cut the wrong one? It did not seem complex. I ran my hand lightly along one, following it from clock to mine. Could it really be this simple to disarm? I looked back to where the man was crouching to see him holding my notebook up with the words, "If you're determined to die down here with me, you should at least tell me what you know about the bombings."

You first, I thought, watching as he turned the notebook back his way to write again. I would never trust an agent of the British Intelligence Service again. My fingers found a wire wound in a loop and I refocused on it rather than the man a few feet away. The loop went round a small screw in the mine and I unwound it carefully it so that it came loose in my fingers. The wire dropped free of the bomb it was attached to and I let out my breath. I followed the wires back to their respective clocks, unwinding the loops one at a time, noticing that Lancaster had caught on and mimicked my actions. We met under the clock where we started from, where four wires now hung loosely from their clocks' backs, all detached from the bombs.

I reached up to take hold of the clock closest to me, glancing at the agent. He lit a cigarette and nodded as if I was plucking an apple from a tree rather than taking our lives into my hand. I wondered for a second how it feels to be that confident, and then I remembered, it's how I used to feel before losing half my powers of deduction. I gritted my teeth as I pulled the clock from its cradle.

CHAPTER 14

"THIS IS RIDICULOUS," I said again.

The men sitting across from me glanced my way — Lancaster with a look of curiosity, the other with annoyance. Who knows what I had said in my confused patois. The evidence and my satchel had been stripped from me, slung over the back of this interrogator's chair, so I had no notebook or pen with which to communicate. Not that these two seemed interested in what I might have to say; their rumbling conversation sounded like an argument to my injured ears.

I was in a holding room of some kind, with a single door and no windows. Not at Scotland Yard, but on the south end of London, if my perception of all the twists and turns we took as I sat in the back of the unmarked lorry was right. I should add a compass to my belt of tools that already includes a folding magnifying glass and a lock pick. This room was stark and old with yellowing walls, and when I concentrated, I could smell old paint … perhaps this was part of a warehouse or a factory. There were no grinding sounds that I could discern and the few men we had passed as I was shuffled into this room had been professionals, of the same ilk as the men in front of me.

After I had walked up the stairs carrying the clock, we had been "escorted" out of The Trifle by five men through a back door into an alley and hustled into the back of a lorry. I could sense Lancaster protesting physically behind me, but we were given no chance to explain or escape and I saw no one else in the alley who could help us, not even one of my faithful Irregulars.

I blew out my breath, remembering Olsen's advice, and refocused on the annoyed man with the moustache and the circular glasses and skin so pale that the red spots of anger in his cheeks looked like poppies. Late fifties, former military if his haircut, scars, and posture were any indication. He held a series of coloured index cards in his hand and seemed to be referring to them as he argued. His lips were almost impossible to read because of the moustache, so I looked at Lancaster's perfectly shaped brown lips instead, catching every third word or so. She. Heddy? Over?

Lancaster suddenly stood up, gesticulating in my direction and knocked over his chair in his exit from the room. He didn't even look back at me.

The older gentleman leaned over to right the chair and when he came back up, the index cards were gone, secreted into his jacket pocket. He cracked his knuckles and met my eyes before speaking directly to me for the first time since escorting me into the room. I understood nothing and pantomimed using a pen and paper, pointing at my satchel behind him.

He frowned, waggling his finger at me, and repeated the pattern of sounds he had said before.

Why would I lie about this?

I slowly redid the pantomime. Maybe he was dull-witted.

My third time through this act, he grabbed my upper arm and shook me, his tone recognizably louder and more threatening, even if the actual words continued to evade me. He put the clock I had detached from the bomb on the table between us and said something I couldn't decipher.

"I don't understand!" I said, annoyingly aware that my words were probably not the ones I intended to say. "Please, if you give me back my pen and paper, I could explain!"

This just seemed to make him angrier and he pulled me upright, now yelling straight into my face. If he intended to scare me, he failed, because all my frustration poured out of me and I yelled back. I shouted about the unfairness of my situation and the injustice in scooping me off the streets of London like a common criminal. I shoved at the man and he gave no ground. That's how Lancaster found us, now both red in the face and panting at the exertion of yelling and not being understood. Carrying a file folder, he spoke to the mustached man as he entered the room. The mustached man shook his head, touching his firearm as he spoke and I instinctively backed up, not understanding the words, but not liking the implication of escalating violence. Lancaster stepped between us, throwing the file on the table. I looked longingly at the open door, wondering how far I would get if I just bolted from the room, leaving these two to argue in my wake. I had convinced myself to at least give it a try when the mustached man moved to pull his gun from his holster and Lancaster gave up verbal negotiation and slammed his fist into the mustached man's cheek.

The man collapsed into a boneless heap at our feet. Lancaster only lingered long enough to ascertain that he was in no condition to follow us before running to the door to look down the hallway. I crouched over the man, made sure he was still breathing, and reached into his pocket, pulling out the coloured index cards. I read details of my life listed next to confirmation dates, more than I thought the Service knew about me, including who my grandparents were. My grandmother was on a different card than the late Irene Adler, so I hoped against hope that her criminal identity hadn't been discovered. The final card detailed the story Annie and Henry Rees were chasing about the stockpiled weapons — according to this card the rumours may be true. I tucked the index cards into my bra; this information was leaving with me today.

I threw my satchel on and took the last two steps to where Lancaster stood in the doorway. He grabbed my hand, pulling me down a hallway lined with closed doors and with exposed plumbing in the ceiling, confirming the warehouse details of this location. We ran down this hallway and then another and a third before we encountered his peers. Lancaster went around a corner, I heard sounds that sounded like hard slaps, and when he jumped back, I saw the reason why. Dark bullet holes had appeared in the wall opposite the hallway. I logged that gunshots sounded like slaps to my damaged ears as I looked up at the ceiling and pulled him towards the stairs that I knew existed behind the door, based on the pattern of pipes, or the lack thereof. We pelted up the stairs, Lancaster leading us until the slapping sound resumed and he stumbled, a red hole appearing at the edge of the white shirt he was wearing. I looked back to see that yes, men were shooting at us from a staircase down and one of them had hit his mark. I pulled Lancaster along the last few floors to the rooftop, the men closing in on us. I pushed Lancaster through the metal door, slammed it shut behind us, holding it against our pursuers. Luckily, Lancaster picked up a metal strut from the rooftop and, with his help, I crammed it against the door handle, buying us a bit of time. I tripped over a half-finished lunch, and beer bottles rolled away from me. This rooftop was littered with refuse.

I backed away from the metal door, watching it shake as men tried to gain access to the roof — and to us — and then looked over the side of the building, seeing the Thames on this side, and streets I did not recognize on the other. Damnit, I left the clock downstairs. My only piece of evidence was in the hands of these idiots.

I turned to see Lancaster buckling on a large backpack. His hands were shaking and his face was pale but determined. Where he had pulled the backpack from, I knew not, but he threw a glance at the door and stepped up and onto the ledge of the building, looking down at me with expectation. I picked up a mostly empty bottle of whisky, gulped down the last dregs, rolled up the index cards, and tucked them into the empty bottle, shoving it into my satchel. We leapt at the water, the taste of whisky burning down my throat as we fell.

He deployed his parachute immediately, needing to because of the minimal height of this five-storey building, especially with my additional weight. I would have slipped out of his arms at the jolt had he not wrapped his legs around mine. We floated out over the river, men running to watch our descent from the banks. We were entirely in the hands of the wind and all the hoping and wishing in the world wouldn't save us from our icy denouement.

Lancaster was tightly buckled into the parachute's canvas straps and the current of the Thames threatened to pull us apart. He fumbled with the buckles, gasping for air as the current dunked him under mercilessly. His hands became desperate, panicky. I held onto his straps with one hand and took a deep breath, giving into the pull of the river. Underwater, I opened my eyes to see Lancaster's head lolling on his chest, his arms floating uselessly in the murky water. I pushed my arm through the strap and dug into his pocket for the knife he had once held against me. By the time I sliced us free of the parachute, I was starting to see black spots in front of my eyes that were not the rubbish usually found in the Thames. My lungs burning, I kicked to the surface as the parachute shot away from us, finally free to embrace the current fully.

Somehow, I pulled Lancaster to shore underneath a bridge I did not recognize in the darkness.

My teeth were chattering so hard I was sure someone would hear them. I could see boats out on the water, the wavering lights of their lanterns shifting over the Thames as they searched for us. Kneeling beside Lancaster I felt a very faint pulse in his neck and he coughed feebly, rolling onto his side at my attentions. My eyes now accustomed to the dark and free of muddy river water, I spied curious observers staring at us from under the bridge. We had nothing worth stealing, but our location was certainly worth a coin or two to the men pursuing us.

"Can you stand?" I whispered down at the man struggling to stand up.

He pushed himself upright with my help and gaining street level, I almost smiled, recognizing the area. That recognition gave me new strength and we made our way down a long alleyway, Lancaster heavy on my shoulder. We avoided the main roads thanks to my memorization of my grandfather's map that detailed the back alleys of London. There! I finally saw our destination ahead. I led Lancaster around the side of the house to where, as I suspected, the light was on in the garage. I propped Lancaster against the garage door, knocked, and hoped for the best.

CHAPTER 15

I WOKE UP IN THE passenger seat of a Rolls-Royce. I was wrapped in blankets, leaning against the window, and when I looked over my shoulder I could see Lancaster lying prostrate in the back seat. Shirtless, so I could see the large bandages that had been wound around him last night, but obviously breathing, he looked slightly better than when I had fallen asleep. The creaking sound of someone opening the garage door made me duck down, but, thankfully, it was someone I could trust. And he was carrying a pen and a dry notebook. He wrote something in the notepad and handed it to me through the open car window.

"I wish you would have come and stayed in the house with me," my friend Beans had written. The good professor was the latest dear friend whom I had now involved in this insane caper.

"What could you have said to Lady Grace by way of explanation?" I wrote back, before manoeuvring my way out of the car with a barely suppressed wince.

"She ... I ...," Beans stuttered, his lips betraying his indecision.

Not sure if he was more embarrassed that I'd surmised that his fiancée was asleep upstairs, or by the fact that he couldn't come up with a quick lie, I took the notebook to write, "I would never ask you to lie to your betrothed. We will be gone as soon as Lancaster is able to leave."

Beans shook his head adamantly, saying something that came out in a rumbling jumble before remembering I couldn't understand him. "When is the last time you ate?" he wrote on the pad.

I shrugged. The afternoon before, surely. He promised to return, exiting the garage the way he had come.

I heard a light rumble from behind me, signalling that Lancaster was awake. He sat up in the car, managing to look roguish despite the gunshot wound and near-drowning. He leaned out the Rolls-Royce window, reaching for the notepad I was holding. His arms were well-muscled and lean, matching his wide chest, with very little hair on either.

"Where are we?"

"My friend Henry's home in Piccadilly."

"You let your friend stitch me up?"

"He's a coroner as well as a professor."

"Perfect," he said aloud, throwing up his arms.

"Why are the British Secret Intelligence Service chasing us?"

Lancaster frowned reading that question. "Because I helped you escape that holding cell. Lucky that I knew that location and that we keep parachutes and weapons on that rooftop or we might not have made it. They think you are behind the bombings."

Rolling my eyes, I wrote, "That much is clear, if entirely without foundation. But why did they nick us at The Trifle? Why not Éamon O'Duffy?"

He didn't look surprised at my question or my knowledge that he was following O'Duffy, but chose not to answer directly. "Colonel Kell is the most suspicious man you will ever meet," Lancaster wrote. "He doesn't trust the Yard, he doesn't trust the government. He thinks you're working with whoever is behind all of this. Your friend Annie's interest in black market weapons she thinks the British government is stockpiling adds to his suspicion."

I picked up the whisky bottle from where I'd placed it on the car's dashboard last night, pulling the index cards free.

"If you're wondering if those are the only copies, yes, I suspect they are," Lancaster wrote, eyeing the cards. "But Kell has an incredible memory, so he's not likely to forget you or me."

"Why did you hit him? He wasn't really going to shoot me, was he?"

Lancaster shrugged, and then wrote, "Threatening a woman is something I can't stomach," as Beans struggled his way under the garage door carrying a tray.

He looked at Lancaster leaning out the window of his Rolls-Royce, shirtless, and me holding a whisky bottle and index cards, and the tray trembled in his hands. I took the tray before my friend could drop the contents — as he was apt to do — putting it down on a workbench and pouring a cup of tea for each of us, hearing the two men's rumblings but not understanding anything.

Beans tapped me on the shoulder with the notepad, "Secret Intelligence Service?" he had written on the page.

"That's the only thing I believe that comes out of his mouth," I wrote back before stuffing biscuits into my mouth ungracefully.

Lancaster leaned out of the car further to see what I had written and I unabashedly held it up for him to read. If he thought I trusted him because of the events of last night, he was sorely mistaken. He grinned in response, receding into the car's backseat to search for his shirt. His back was a perfect model of masculine beauty but for two old bullet wounds in his shoulder, scars I had to force myself to look away from.

"Michaels has the Yard scouring London for you. We must go there straight away," Beans wrote, tapping me on the shoulder, pulling my gaze away from the annoying agent. Beans handed me the notepad and then turned to pull a much cleaner shirt of his own out of a cupboard in the garage. He passed it to the agent with a scowl, saying something I could not understand.

"What about Brian?" I wrote. Surely my partner was searching for me.

Beans glanced down at the floor of his garage before writing, "I have not seen him in a few weeks. He's been rather absent from the Yard since the incident at the train station."

That niggling feeling that started when Michaels pointed out Brian's lateness was growing to alarm now.

"What aren't you telling me?" I wrote.

Instead of answering, Beans shook his head, dismissing my question, or evading it. I had barely had a moment to think of Brian or poor Annie since I was nicked, but the guilt hit me like a blow to the stomach, complete with nausea. I wished I could at least pick up a phone and tell them I was safe, but I had the verbal communication abilities of a toddler at present.

The shirt fit the agent like a glove, his fingers deftly doing the buttons up over the bandage Beans had applied to his gunshot wound.

"We can't go to the Yard," Lancaster said, speaking slowly enough for me to understand the words on his lips.

Of course he didn't want us to go to the police; that would put a stop to this cloak-and-dagger drama spies seemed to love. I ignored him, writing to Beans instead, "I hate to involve you any more than you already are. Can you please ring up the Yard and have a car sent down for us?"

Lancaster stepped between us to take the notepad and write, "If you go to the Yard, you will put your friends in danger."

A low blow that underlined just how well the Secret Intelligence Service knew me.

"Why should we believe you?" I wrote on a pad of paper. Beans must have asked a similar question because Lancaster addressed us both.

"Kell suspects Scotland Yard's involvement in the bombing," Lancaster replied. "It's why Portia became a prime suspect so easily. Best to lay low. Maybe even get out of London for a while."

All three of us whirled towards the garage door — I heard that knock! Lancaster leapt for my hand and pulled me behind the Rolls. Beans, wide-eyed and worried, ducked under the garage door, smacking his head on the way out.

Lancaster grasped my face. "We have to go. Now."

Everything in me rebelled against the idea of leaving, but it seemed true, that I was putting my friends in danger. Under the garage door, I could see three pairs of men's shoes. The brown ones were new and polished to a shine; the black ones scuffed and too small a size for the man wearing them. An ill-match that spoke of a collaboration between high and low. Lancaster tugged on my hand and I allowed myself to be pulled to the window at the back of the garage. I still intended to get to Scotland Yard, but Beans did not need to be further ensnarled.

I had one leg through the open window when I saw Beans' face reappear through the small gap under garage door. He was laid out on his belly, being forcefully handcuffed. He turned his face my way to mouth "Go!" and then he was hauled out of my eye line again.

CHAPTER 16

"WE CAN'T STAY HERE much longer," read the note Lancaster tossed in front of me as he passed my table. Surrounded by piles of books in the very back room of the oldest library in London, I was going back and forth between old newspapers and the single lip-reading manual to be found on the stacks and Lancaster was orbiting the bookshelves like a caged tiger. He was going to reopen his wound if he didn't stop that.

I held up the note I'd written a half hour ago in answer, "You're welcome to leave at any time."

In our escape from Beans' home, I could not convince Lancaster to stop at a police box to ring up Scotland Yard, but I did run into one of my Baker Street Irregulars. She goggled at the man I was with and he just grinned down at her, casually putting his arm over my shoulder. I gave her a few coins to pass on this location to Brian.

Thanks to the newspapers, I could confirm that Éamon O'Duffy was well-known to the police, having been brought in for questioning eight times in six years for everything from public nuisance charges to suspicion of terrorist activity. He declared his motives at regular intervals in front of crowds of Londoners: self-rule for Ireland. He had defended brothers-

in-arms, marched in protest in front of Scotland Yard, and orga-
nized rallies in response to Parliamentary acts. He was all over
the British newspapers. But as much as I had postulated that
the bomber would stay close to a bomb site to watch the drama
unfold, would he actually sit so comfortably above his weapons
after they had been placed? I needed more data. I needed Brian
to speak to the man. So here I would wait until we could combine
our data and figure a way out of this mess. I couldn't hear Lancaster's steps on the hardwood floor, but I knocked on the
wooden desk where I was seated and once again, had to smile
at hearing it so clearly. I was no doctor, but the data seemed to
suggest that my ears — my left more than my right — were healing.

Speaking of data, I wrote a note for Lancaster for his next
orbital pass.

"Since we're here till Brian arrives, why don't you tell me
what the Secret Intelligence Service knows about Heddy Collins?"

The spy reluctantly picked up the pencil to write back. "They
know nothing because she's no one. Widow to Major Collins
who was killed in Ireland in one of their internal scuffles. She
works at Downing Street and seemed to be of interest to you
the day we met there."

He had still been in the crowd when I bumped into Mrs.Collins
outside Downing Street. Damnit.

"How do you know her?"

His hand hesitated over the notepad and then he wrote: "The
Major and I had dealings during the uprisings and afterwards."

"Dealings? Good or bad?"

Lancaster put down the pen, a steeliness coming over his face
in his clenched jaw and the way his shoulders stiffened.

"Is she capable of the bombings?" I asked, changing tacks.

He shook his head immediately, making me suspect that the dealings had had as much to do with the Mrs. as the Major. An affair, perhaps?

"What of her daughter?"

"The Collinses had no children," Lancaster wrote back. "And Heddy never remarried. Heddy has no motive, no skills in bomb-making, and the only link you have for her is seeing her at Downing Street where she had all the reason to be."

I didn't share my information about the gun in her purse or the young girl at the college who hadn't flinched at the explosion that dropped everyone around her to the ground. Her resemblance to Heddy might have been a coincidence, but eliminating Heddy as a suspect did not eliminate the girl. Also, I had this niggling idea about the queen's lady-in-waiting and her hands. I doubted her injuries were specifically related to this case and the bombings, but something about her made me suspicious. And my brain wouldn't let it go.

Lancaster had meanwhile returned to his circuit, so it was by pure luck that I saw the figure steal into the library because I surely would not have heard them if he didn't.

Even if I hadn't recognized the person through their disguise of a borrowed coat and covered hair, the bloodhound tugging at its leash gave them away. Plus, I recognized the gait — slightly favouring the left foot because the heel of the right boot was wobbly and needed to be replaced. I waved at Lancaster, but his back was turned as he walked in the opposite direction from our visitors, who were ducking behind bookcases as they made their way to my table.

Despite the slapstick humour of this approach, I did not want to trigger a replay of the knife-to-the-throat introduction Lancaster seemed to favour, so I wrote a seven word note, wrapped it around the pencil and with the use of one of the rubber bands on the table, launched it at the bookcase our visitor was hiding behind.

My aim must have been decent because less than a minute later, Annie stepped out from behind the bookcase, pulling the hat off her head. "Who the devil is Lancaster?"

The devil himself stepped from the shadows behind Annie, causing her to jump back. Nerissa, who was at Annie's feet, showed her teeth. Annie backed up to my table, pulling Nerissa with her, keeping her eyes on the spy, a steady stream of conversation evident in the way his lips were moving. Neither of them were looking at me so they couldn't see my smile. I was hearing more and more of their words. Still quieter in volume than usual, but actual words.

I didn't know how she found us until she pulled a familiar piece of paper out of her pocket. She had intercepted the note I had meant to get to Brian. The question (which I scrawled down quickly) was why?

Lancaster seemed to accept whatever verbal explanation Annie had provided for her arrival and slipped back between the bookshelves. For a tall man, he moved like a trained dancer, fluid and smooth. Only then did Nerissa drop her suspicious stance and hurl herself into my arms to cover my face in slurpy kisses.

"He ... be sure I ... followed," Annie said, her face finally turned my way, her lips enunciating each word carefully for me before taking my notepad from me to frown down at my question about Brian.

"Brian was still abed when I left Baker Street," she wrote as I gave Nerissa as much love as I could. "A late night, according to his mother."

The unsettled feeling in my stomach bubbled to a higher intensity boil and I wrote back, "Pursuing a new lead at the Yard?"

"I couldn't get a decent word out of him, to be honest," she wrote. "He's no help to either of us."

"Either of us? Your father?"

Annie blinked tears from her eyes before writing with a slightly shakier hand. "I still haven't heard directly from him, but his landlord in Sandwell said he hadn't been home in a week. I couldn't get a clearer answer from the man before I ran out of money for the call."

I pushed aside my growing unease about my partner, scratching behind Nerissa's ears to reassure us both. "We'll go to the bank right now and get enough money to make all the calls you need."

"You can't go out in public," she replied, then pulled out a crumpled-up piece of paper and put it on the desk in front of me. I straightened out the poster paper to read the words "People of Interest" in bold above a photo of Ian Lancaster and Portia Constance Adams. A phone number I didn't recognize was listed below and Nerissa picked her head off my lap to growl at the stacks. Lancaster was back to drag us out of the library building.

CHAPTER 17

"FORTY QUID SHOULD BE enough," Lancaster said, his arm buried elbow-deep in a wall cavity just outside Barrows Cemetery.

Annie shook her head at me and spoke, "How can I think of leaving you with a ... spy?"

I didn't catch whatever adjective she was using to describe the spy a few feet away from where we hid, but I wrote her an answer. "You've already been taken in for questioning by Box 850 once, plus I need you to check on Beans and Brian. And you have to think of your family — your father and your brothers."

She grasped me by the shoulders. "You're my family as much as them, Portia."

I felt like I could almost hear the words she said, and I hugged her to me, surprising her because I was not one for hugging. She meant what she said, of course. She had done her best to locate my grandmother before meeting me at the library, anticipating my worry for her. What Annie did not know was that no one needed to worry about Irene Adler. If there was one thing she was an expert at, it was evading the law. She would find me before the Yard or Box 850 found her, of that much I was sure.

"Can you tell me anything else about the weapons stockpiling?" I wrote. "Did you learn anything from the diplomats?"

Annie pulled me a little further away as if Lancaster would read over our shoulder and wrote, "Only that there is some backdoor trading happening and the Germans and Austrians are not pleased. Someone is trying to keep them out of the room when talks are happening. Austria sent a delegation of negotiators to try to keep the peace."

"Who is selling the arms?"

"I don't know that it's a government," Annie wrote. "Henry thinks it's a private sale rather than a country. But we're talking millions of pounds of weapons. That's too much for one person to have. It's like our government thinks we're going to war again."

"Looking at the state of nationalism and the kinds of men being elected to the east of us, I think anything is possible," I wrote back, the uneasy feeling settling in my stomach for what felt like a long stay.

"And meanwhile, I'm leaving you with," Annie wrote, followed by a large arrow pointing to the man smoking a few feet away.

"I have Nerissa and we have a plan," I wrote. "We will meet at Charing Cross Station two days hence and if either of us does not show up, we go straight to Scotland Yard, regardless of who knows what or who is threatened with arrest. If one of us is unreachable for whatever reason, we put an ad in *The Lady* for a nanny with the code I taught you."

Annie's mouth formed an "O" of surprise and she reached into her voluminous borrowed coat to pull out a large packet. Speaking, she said, "Your pills. They were … on the downstairs side table, outside the Dawes' flat. I … them … way out the door."

She held them out to me and then thought better of it, pushing the packet back into the coat pocket, shaking the coat off her shoulders and throwing it around me instead.

As I had been deprived of my coat since being accosted at

The Trifle, this was especially appreciated and made me squeeze her again.

"Here," said Lancaster, pressing the cash into Annie's hands. "We should be on our way as well."

That hole in the wall held more than just money; the spy was now wearing a newsboy hat and he placed a pair of clear cat-eye-shaped glasses on my face. I looked around him at the brick wall that he had restored to its previously plain facade and decided this was a trick I could learn from Box 850 — hiding disguises and aids in different spots all over London.

Annie did not look ready to leave, even when Lancaster gifted her with one of his "trust me, I'm too pretty to be bad" smiles. She responded by jabbing a finger into his chest, saying something to him that made the smile slide off his face like a slick of oil off a shiny hubcap, and stalking off down the alleyway. She glanced back once, meeting my gaze, before stepping out onto the sidewalk and then she was gone.

"Loyal friend," he remarked, sliding his arm around my waist as if we were lovers looking for a quiet spot and pushing the glasses up the bridge of my nose with his other hand. "Where to now, Detective?"

I was ready for that question, having already answered it in an earlier conversation with Annie. I raised my notebook between us and pointed to it on my page. "Now we find the bomber."

⇌

"JUST BECAUSE WE CAN'T see them, doesn't mean they're not staking out the place," Lancaster wrote, forced to resort to the pad because he was whispering and refused to stop chain smoking. I pulled the packet out of my pocket, noting its size. The nurse had delivered at least a month's worth of pills. Perhaps they had gotten tired of the daily deliveries. Or perhaps they had given up on my recovery and this was just my life now. Medicated to the gills. I slipped four pills under my tongue, observing they tasted slightly more bitter than usual, and noticed the smaller pills in another package. These weren't mine. These were Brian's, damnit. Now he was without his medication, which he could neither afford to replace nor afford to miss.

Lancaster reached for one of Brian's pills and said something I couldn't decipher. He pulled out his cigarette to say it again, "Opium." I looked back down at the small pill, not liking the quick identification, but also running through Brian's symptoms in my head, comparing those to this treatment plan. I wished I had access to Watson's myriad medical notebooks on the bookshelves of my flat. Or Gavin's quick mind when it came to chemicals. He had been a boon to Scotland Yard as a coroner, specializing in poisons and unexplainable deaths. It's one of the things that had first attracted me to him — that quick mind.

Dragging my attention back to the present was difficult. We were hiding in a train car near where all my recent troubles had begun, the police cordon still wrapped around trees and rubble, the darkness almost absolute because no one had administered to the streetlamps since the explosion. Nerissa and Lancaster had reached a détente that required that the bloodhound place her body between ours. Her level of trust in the spy mimicked mine and, as always, I appreciated our synergy, but I could still feel Lancaster's breath on my neck and the smell of his cigarettes combined with his natural scent into something wholly unique to him. I wanted to label it unpleasant, but couldn't quite manage it.

Meanwhile, three cases wrestled for position in my mind: Brian's withdrawal since his injury, Annie's missing father, and this ruddy bomber who, by remaining at large, was keeping me from dealing with the other two cases. Annie was chasing the weapons-stockpiling angle, but it really didn't help that I was unable to operate out in the open.

"This is the bomber's first and most amateur target and therefore is likely to hold the most clues," I wrote, handing the notebook to Lancaster before leaning over to look through the slightly open door of the train car.

Lancaster was watching for Kell's men or patrolling constables from the Yard. His declared motivation was much plainer — to clear our names so he could return to his nefarious day job — and that required getting a hold of Kell or one of his men and convincing them of our innocence on our turf rather than theirs.

I was watching for someone altogether different. Nerissa was curled on her side, fast asleep. Until she wasn't. She picked up her head, her ears rotating like sonars.

"There," I said, tugging on Lancaster's arm and pointing at the thickset body that had stolen into the train yard. If he was surprised, it didn't show on his face as he slid the door open an inch wider for us to see out. I whispered to Nerissa to stay quiet and we lay flat on our bellies, side by side, watching as the person snuck closer to us, sliding between train cars demonstrating a familiarity with the scene that identified them before I saw their face.

"Oy," the man squawked as Lancaster hopped up from his prone position to grab him by the lapels. Nerissa leapt out of the train car, growling up at the man.

"He's the driver," I said, recognizing the man trying to wriggle out of his grasp. This was a remarkably tidy presentation, his pants mended but pressed, his hair neat as a pin. Not the sot I was expecting at all.

Lancaster said something, surprise registering on his face,

but I couldn't understand his words. He pulled the man into the train car, and turned to me, enunciating carefully. "You spoke."

I shrugged, but he grasped me by the shoulders, "You said 'He's the driver.'"

My mouth fell open in surprise. I had been expecting that my words were their usual jumble of randomness, it seemed too much to hope that my speech would return at the same time as my hearing. The driver had scrambled to his knees, but Nerissa's growling kept him from attempting to escape his situation.

Lancaster was not playing the nice cop in this scenario, keeping a strong hold on the man, and badgering him with minimally worded questions that generated minimal responses like "Gerroff me," or something like that, perhaps with the addition of a cuss word that slandered the spy's ethnicity. Lancaster drew back a fist and that seemed to be enough hardball for this man. I had my hand on Nerissa's back so I could feel when she stopped growling, the vibrations receding along her lean body. I grabbed for my notebook.

The man licked his lips. "I work here ... explain nothing ... you two."

"This station is closed," I said, hoping I was still understood. "You're not here to fix the trains dressed up like you are. Why are you here this late?"

The man's eyes darted around the darkened space outside our train car and I figured out the reason for his combination of skittishness and immaculate dress. He was meeting someone of the female persuasion. Someone he was not supposed to be meeting at all.

"How long have you been stepping out on your wife, Digby?" I said.

He practically leapt out of Lancaster's grasp then, demonstrating that my words were still coming out as planned. The men scuffled for control, but Nerissa had turned her attention to someone else entering our vicinity. Someone was walking around the train cars in the darkness. At least, that's what Nerissa's reaction was telling me.

I didn't want to scare the new arrival, but my bloodhound had no such forethought, darting out of the train car, nose pointed right at the intruder.

With a curse, I took off after her. Nerissa's barks were sharper sounds to my ears than human voices, but in the darkness, I could neither visually follow her lithe body nor hear her barks to follow her as she chased the person around the damaged train yard. Still at a full run, I rummaged in my satchel for my torch and tripped over some rail tracks, landing on my elbows with a yelp of pain. That's where Nerissa found me, choosing to abandon her quarry at the fear her mistress was in trouble.

"Sorry, girl," I said as she wrapped herself around me, checking for injuries. She dropped a piece of fabric at my feet as she licked my face, and I picked it up, flashing my torch on it. Unless I was very mistaken, it was from a woman's thin cotton dress. Cheap and worn, like the clothing I had worn for my first two decades when I lived in Toronto, and much too thin for the weather.

Lancaster's torch came bobbing along the tracks, locating us at last. He was dragging a very reluctant Harold Digby by the arm.

"Whoever she is, you were unwise to keep this as your rendezvous spot after the explosion," I said up at the two men. Lancaster nodded, a small smile on his face, having understood my words. "Is she also married?"

Digby's eyes searched for the woman who had evaded Nerissa and she turned to growl up at him menacingly, as if warning him not to try to run because she would not let another escape.

"Or is she perhaps not a paramour," I mused aloud, struggling to my feet, my torch light aimed at Digby's clean clothes, "but a long-lost daughter?"

CHAPTER 18

DIGBY'S PLACE IN BAYSWATER was a run-down townhouse that presented far too much physical evidence of hoarding and solitary drinking to be lived in by anyone but a bachelor. Digby pulled two mismatched chairs up to his kitchen table and poured us all a small glass of homebrew. I had to force myself to turn away from the clues to the man's life laid starkly before me: the former wife, the unpaid bills, the mother who had lived here before him, their relationship that had soured his marriage.

I shook my head, downing the drink down in a single swallow and grimacing. It needed sugar, but that was an expensive luxury Digby obviously couldn't afford.

"My wife left with my wee girl when I was at my worst," Harold explained, knitting and unknitting his hands as he spoke. "The drink got to me. I was the last one left amongst my mates with a job, and my mum, well, she …," he trailed off here, as if used to being stopped at this point. Finding no one to interrupt him, "My mum, she died. And I just took it up again. And Val, she had it. She left with our little girl, Ilsa."

I was able to understand most of what Digby said and Lancaster was good enough to answer my few questions directly.

"But that must have been several years ago," I said in response. Lancaster frowned at me, shaking his head, so I wrote it down, swallowing past my resentment that my speech issues persisted.

"More than ten, yes, and I tried — I swear I did — to clean up my act, but Val, she wouldn't hear of it," he replied, taking another swig of his moonshine, as I leaned closer with my left ear. "I got a job and started sending them money. And then, all of a sudden, the money was getting sent back."

"When was that?" I wrote.

"She left me in … must have been '22," Digby said. "The money started coming back about five years later I think. I don't know. Those are hazy days to be honest."

"Val moved?" Lancaster asked.

Digby shook his head, "No, Val needed my money, couldn't work after the war and all, because of her German family. Val must have died poor thing. Because next thing I know, our little girl's left at the orphanage. Except by the time I found that out, Ilsa wasn't there. She'd run away. And everywhere I looked, she wasn't."

"How did you find her then?" I wrote on my notepad.

"She found me," he answered, his eyes going wide at the memory. "Just showed up at the train yard, bold as brass, looking just like my Val when I met her. Wanted to know why I abandoned her and where her mother was."

I bumped my glass with my knuckles and cursed, reaching for some old newspapers on the table to absorb the spilled liquid. "Does your daughter have two different coloured eyes, Digby?"

"Yes, just like my Val," he replied.

"But what happened when you finally spoke to Ilsa?" Lancaster pressed.

"She was so angry, so … unforgiving," Digby replied, wringing his hands. "I couldn't make her understand that Val had left me and that I had tried to find her. I would never have left her at an orphanage."

Lancaster gave me an I-told-you-so look before asking, "What did she want?"

"Nothing, as far as I could tell," Digby said. "And she wouldn't take anything from me, not a thing."

He refilled his glass and Lancaster's. I put my hand over my own glass and through the clear bottom of my glass I noticed a photo in the wet newspaper. Was that ... Gavin? I dragged the paper out from the wetness, trying to smooth the paper down. It was *The Scotsman*, a newspaper I didn't usually read. Digby must have gotten a copy on his train travels and it was a month old.

The caption was hard to read, but it was about the arrival of a new Austrian ambassador in Edinburgh. Yes, my former boyfriend had returned. He had left two years ago on a teaching tour sponsored by the Austrians and now he was travelling with an ambassador? This must be the Austrian delegation Annie was referring to. Why hadn't this been reported in the London newspapers?

Lancaster put a hand on my arm and I glanced up at him, my brain full of questions.

"The night before the explosion at the train station," I wrote, refocusing with difficulty, "you had a drink."

He eyed his glass of homebrew before answering, as if negotiating with himself, and then pushed it aside.

"I was nervous. I thought I'd gotten rid of all my hooch, but I found a bottle under the driver's seat that night. Must have been one of the other boys'. Barely half left, but I drank it down, to give myself a bit of courage. I shouldn't have."

"What happened when Ilsa got there?" Lancaster asked.

"She didn't," Digby said, shaking his head. "She never showed up, though I stayed all night and fell asleep where I sat. I only woke up when the train car started moving and then it hit the platform and I was thrown clear."

"Did you see anyone else?" Lancaster pressed. "A man? Early forties? Muttonchops too long to be fashionable? He might have been with a few mates."

Digby shook his head, "I woulda said something if I had. Would have gotten me out of the Yard sooner if I'd had someone to name, but there was no one, I swear."

"What about tonight?" I asked, tapping the notebook.

"My Ilsa, she sent this note this morning," Digby said, digging in his pants pocket and pulling out a crumpled piece of paper. "Said I was to meet her tonight. That she needed money and that I owed her for ruining her life. And now, you've gone and scared her off."

"If she needs money, she'll be back," Lancaster said as I reached for the note, holding it to my nose and recognizing a faint chemical smell. I read it, then handed it to the spy so I could write my final words for Digby.

"We need you to tell us when she reaches out again, Digby."

"Why should I?" he replied, his answer clear on his lips and the way his shoulders came up, defensive and suspicious.

"Because the first time you met she didn't want money and suddenly now she does. She's not coming to you for money," I wrote. "She's coming to finish what she started. To kill you."

CHAPTER 19

"SHE'S NOT THE BOMBER," Lancaster said, leaning against the doorframe.

I had spent the last five minutes circling the single bed in the room, ending up by the window where I could look out and see Digby smoking on his stoop. Nerissa had the opposite reaction, jumping onto the bed and curling up as if she had solved the world's problems and could now rest easy. I guess the dried sausage Digby had scrounged up really did solve all canine worries.

"Portia," Lancaster said, coming over to stand beside me, causing my bloodhound's eyes to narrow slightly. "We can't waste time on this girl. Nor the lady's maid. This bomber is not who you think it is."

"WE don't have to waste time at all," I wrote. "As always, the door is right there, and you are welcome to take it. I have a lead, I conveniently have bait standing out there smoking his heart out, and once I have her in custody, I will be able to get back to my normal life."

Lancaster took the notebook and pen out of my hand. "Normal life?"

I dropped my eyes at the reminder, reaching into my satchel for my pills. "My new normal," I muttered, popping the pills into my mouth. It reminded me that I still needed to get Brian's medicine back to him, but I couldn't risk doing it myself because of the posters Kell had up all around London and I couldn't let Digby out of my sight for fear that he'd either escape us or be killed by his vengeful daughter. I still didn't know why she was sending bomb threats to places like Downing Street or Parliament, or how Grey Hall had become a target, but I intended to ask her first chance I got. O'Duffy had the better motive based on the targets, but Ilsa had the better opportunity. I threw down *The Scotsman* in the rubbish bin. I'd read it front to back and found no more mention of Gavin save that caption. What was he doing here?

Digby tossed down his cigarette and came back in the house. I believed him when he said that his daughter sent the two notes she'd written to his townhouse, so as long as he stayed here, waiting for her contact, we were all on the same side. The shit might hit the fan once she'd made contact and he had to decide if he believed me as to her intentions.

I needed a disguise. And I needed this spy to watch Digby. For some reason, I was starting to trust him and according to Nerissa's lack of reaction when he spread his large frame next to hers on the bed, so was my bloodhound.

I kicked off my shoes and joined them, the dog lying between us, facing the door.

"Why are you still trying to get rid of me?" Lancaster said, turning on his side so I could see his lips.

"You're a spy," I answered, via my notebook.

"I've never lied to you," he countered.

"If you were trying to gain my trust, this is exactly the type of scenario that Box 850 would construct. You isolate me from my allies. You demonstrate a willingness to take my side against your employer. You risk your life to save me. It's all a little too convenient."

He read the note and then said, "I could say the same about you. You risked your life to save me in the river. Why didn't you just leave me to die from my wounds? I would have either drowned or bled to death, but in either case, I was in no condition to stop you from escaping."

I glanced down at his wound, visible again now that he'd unbuttoned his borrowed shirt. The bandages had a slight stain of blood, the colour hovering between ochre and red.

"Morality trumps distrust. Or at least it should."

"Is that all it was?" he said slowly, putting his hand on my arm, testing both me and the dog between us. When neither of us bit it off he started rubbing it gently up and down from shoulder to elbow.

Instead of tensing up, I found myself relaxing to his touch, unexpectedly. Drawn into his deep brown eyes almost against my will.

"You shouldn't," I said, knowing that it was a useless statement both in understanding my garbled speech and as a deterrent to what was happening.

Nerissa sat up suddenly between us and leapt to the window to peer down. I rolled that way too and saw Digby steal out of his own backyard.

He'd decided to go it alone. Damn the man!

I grabbed my satchel and ran down the stairs after him, Nerissa leading the way, Lancaster close behind.

I leashed Nerissa as soon as we were able to see the man's back in the moonlight as he ran down the empty London streets. He didn't seem to be trying to hide his escape, in fact, as we turned another corner onto a longer street with working streetlamps, it became clear to me that we were headed to the nearest train yard: Paddington.

Nerissa desperately pulled at her leash. She wanted to overtake the huffing man. I pulled her back. I didn't want to spook the girl again, but I wished Brian was with me instead of Lancaster. I knew Brian's style and he knew mine, we wouldn't need to communicate this intention, but Lancaster ... he was as unpredictable as my bloodhound in this situation.

We made it to the train yard and the three of us stayed in the shadows while Digby fumbled with keys to the main ticket office.

"What if the building is wired to explode?" Lancaster said, on the balls of his feet.

"Unlikely," I said, and then wrote quickly. "Paddington is a busy station and police patrols have been increased at all tube spots since the last explosion. But Ilsa could be waiting to confront her father inside."

"That's a Cardiff goods train waiting at the station, if she's going to make an escape, we need to stop her now," Lancaster said, stepping over to the police call box. I nodded; we were going to be brought in for questioning as well, but as long as that girl was coming with us, I considered that a win. Especially if we were taken in by Scotland Yard where (I hoped) I still had friends.

He made the call, as I watched Digby finally find the right key and apply it to the door. Lancaster had stepped back over to my side when I heard a terrible cry of pain. We ran in unison to the ticket office. I got there last to see Digby holding his daughter's body in his arms, his mouth open as he wailed against what was obvious, the blood around her body and her grey pallor marking that she was well past aid. I forced my eyes away from his despair to survey the ticket room, its benches and ticket booths unremarkable and undisturbed.

Nerissa was sniffing all around the room and Lancaster had stepped to Digby's side, perhaps to console him or more likely to assess the body beside him. I purposefully focused on the body, noting that she been shot at close range if the powder burns on her back were to be believed, her belly a mess of blood and entrails, marking the bullet's trajectory. Her fingers on her left hand looked stained and scratched, but I'd have to get closer to assess them and Digby did not look open to my approach. The fact that she had been shot from behind indicated that she had been surprised by her attacker or that her attacker couldn't look the girl in the face. Nerissa caught my attention hovering in one corner, where I picked up the cartridge she'd been so focused on. It was not a cartridge size I was familiar with, the words PARABELLUM 9MM stamped on the base. The train whistle cut through my observations, as I popped the cartridge in my pocket and checked the door handle, finding no evidence of forced entry. So, either Digby's daughter had her own key or her murderer did.

I turned back to see Digby violently push Lancaster away. He was still cradling his daughter in his right arm and the extent of his grief made it harder to understand him as he slurred and spat curses at us. Lancaster tried to reach for them again and Digby pulled an old service revolver out of his jacket and fired wildly, the sound as loud as I remembered gunfire being. I recoiled, diving left at Nerissa and saw Lancaster dive to the right out of the corner of my eye. When I looked behind me to see where the bullet hit, to my horror, I saw a uniformed officer stagger through the open door.

A sergeant from the local constabulary by the pips on his jacket, he clutched at his throat, the blood already flowing rapidly. His eyes rolled back in his head as Lancaster caught him and lowered him to the ground. I quickly undid the man's collar, but the rush of slick blood stymied my work and the man convulsed twice and lay still.

I pressed both hands to the man's throat, feeling for a pulse, but his throat was a mangle of muscle and bloody tissue. I couldn't feel any pulse through my hands. We had called him here. This was our fault. I closed his nose and breathed air into his mouth but it just whistled wetly out of his throat cavity, not even reaching his chest, which remained still. I looked up at Lancaster desperately, but another sound of a slap snapped our eyes back to Digby.

The carnage was complete. Seeing his daughter dead and then causing the death of an officer must have been too much for the old man. He had pressed the gun to his head and ended this tragedy with a final bullet.

Covered in blood, I looked from body to body to the spy who knelt beside me and knew what we had to do.

CHAPTER 20

HE HAD JUST TURNED *the corner in time to watch them leave together, stepping over a uniformed body in the doorway, the dog following close behind. He wanted to stop them, but he knew that impulse had nothing to do with justice. It was an entirely jealous impulse. Portia led the way to the train, which had started its departure from the station, and he stepped forward, out of the shadows. Could he really let her leave like a thief in the night? She leapt onto the train and he saw something large fall out of her coat pocket. Multiple whistles signalled the arrival of constables at the ticket station, surrounding the body in the doorway, making his decision for him. She had made her bed. She would have to sleep in it without him.*

THE RHYTHMIC MOVEMENT OF the train did nothing to alleviate the tension in my body. Lancaster looked just as bad, sitting on the opposite end of the train car, as far away from Nerissa and me as possible. My bloodhound kept trying to lick my hands, but I couldn't bring myself to let her, so she settled for licking her own paws clean of the blood that had soaked that horrible scene.

I held my hands in front of me, palms up, the blood red drying to maroon that marked me up to my wrists. Almost against my will, I looked down at my dress and satchel, finding with relief that the darkness of both hid the worst of the stains. This wasn't my first murder scene — or my first bloody suicide — so I recognized the adrenaline that had carried me here, but the shock was fading to be replaced by cold calculation. I cast my eyes around the train car, pushing myself up to examine the barrel closest to me. I wrested the top off to find it filled with flour. I dismissed it, opening the next one. This one was filled with what smelled like beer. I scooped handfuls of the liquid, rubbing my hands and wrists to get rid of as much blood as I could. I then tipped over the barrel so no one would be subjected to the dirtied alcohol. Lancaster hadn't moved at all, his arms wrapped around himself defensively. I squatted down beside him.

"What a cock up," he said, turning his dark eyes my way. "SIS will never deal with me now."

"We didn't kill anyone, Lancaster," I said, filing away that admission and speaking with more confidence than I actually felt. "Our mistake was not understanding the stakes. The bomber is feeling boxed in and is acting more and more desperately."

"Bomber?" Lancaster repeated, affirming that at least one of my words had been the one I meant to say and looking down at his bloody hands. "Neither of them were the bomber. We're back at square one and two people are dead."

"If they're not involved, why are they dead?" I challenged him. I pulled out the bullet cartridge I had picked up at the scene. "Do you recognize this? It's not a company I've come across before."

"If you're asking if I've seen it before, sure. It's German, from the war," he replied dismissively. "Common enough amongst our enemies."

Digby was married to a German woman who left him — Val, Ilsa's mother — but he was carrying a British gun. The Digbys are involved, though perhaps not how I originally thought. I needed to write an ad for Annie right away. The death of the sergeant meant that we were on the run until we had the real bomber. I would not be meeting her at Charing Cross.

I sat down and opened my notepad, creating an ad for a nanny, as Annie and I had agreed, incorporating a message about the scene we had just left and encouraging her to write back with news about the queen's lady-in-waiting and whether Parabellum ammunition was part of the weapons story she was writing. Annie and I favoured a modified skip code; the actual message was the first word and then every fourth word of a sentence. Wilans' involvement seemed like even more of a long shot given the murder scene, but my leads were drying up faster than this blood on my dress. Surely Scotland Yard could pursue Éamon O'Duffy in my absence. I added a line about an Irish leader to the ad just in case. Lancaster leaned against me, snoring remarkably for a man who had seemed so troubled moments ago, and Nerissa curled up at my feet. I hesitated and then added a final line about Gavin returning to town, referring to him as Mr. Whitt and hoping Annie would understand whom I was referring to. Whitaker was the smartest person I knew (besides Sherlock Holmes and Irene Adler) and as odd as it would be for him to look for a code in *The Lady*, I wouldn't put it past him. His return couldn't have anything to do with the bombings though. What possible agenda of his could it satisfy? Gavin was driven by power and money, two things that had evaded him growing up in the worst orphanages in London. Other than the power to terrorize, these bombings seemed to hold no power that he would be interested in. Thoughts of his criminal pursuits naturally brought up feelings about my grandmother. Irene Adler had spent five decades stealing from and blackmailing the rich and powerful, evading the law, including my grandfathers. The sooner she found me, the sooner she could help me. It was just a matter of time. Wasn't it?

CHAPTER 21

I WOKE TO THE sunrise peeking around the edges of the large train door.

"Welcome back," said Gavin, startling me from my relaxed position propped against a barrel.

"Gavin," I whispered, struggling to my feet in the moving train. "How did you …? What are you doing here?"

He sat comfortably in the shadows of the train car still unlit by the sun, his suit impeccable and Italian-made, his long legs drawn up so they tented and his arms hung between them.

"I might ask you the same thing," he answered, looking up at me with those eyes that could see so much. His cheekbones were less pronounced than when last I saw him, the Austrians must have fed him well. There was a silver pin on his lapel I didn't recognize, featuring a male lion holding a trident.

"Me?" I demanded, stepping forward and nearly losing my footing as the train seemed to curve around a sharp corner. "I'm chasing a murderer and evading being wrongfully thrown in jail for … what do you have to do with this, anyway?"

"What makes you think I have anything to do with this?"

The train swerved again, and my shoulder took the brunt of it as I hit the wall of the train car.

He didn't stand, or try to help me, and seemed unaffected by the violence of our shared journey.

"This is a dream," I said, ignoring the pain in my shoulder. "That's why you can understand me."

"I always understand you. And I'm not surprised you continue to dream of me," he said, his mouth lifting into that mocking grin I used to love. "I do the same. We are connected. Whether we like it or not."

I squatted down so that my centre of gravity would give me the stability he seemed to have, but felt no more secure. He, on the other hand, looked like he was part of the train car, he moved in unison with the shaking and swerving.

"Dreaming of you means nothing," I replied, dropping to my knees to try crawling closer to him. "I just saw your photo in a newspaper. You're in my mind, but you're not relevant. If you are part of this, I don't see how and I don't see why."

"I don't believe in coincidences," we said in unison.

A particularly hard turn slid me into him and he caught me between his legs, his arms wrapped around me in a way I remembered well and not without fondness. "I'm not the man you should be worried about," he said, softly now, his breath on my face. He kissed my forehead.

I woke with a jolt.

"Who's Gavin?" asked Lancaster from beside me, a question I read from his lips because the silence had returned in my waking state. He looked better for resting, a light line of stubble tracing his jaw, his eyes less sunken. He was eating an apple with one hand and patting Nerissa with his other.

"My ex," I said, experimenting with my speech.

He nodded, reaffirming that my mouth was saying what my

brain wanted it to say. I couldn't count on it remaining, but I would never take that ability for granted again, even if it seemed less reliable than the return of my hearing. I reached into my pocket and was only mildly surprised to find that my package of pills was missing. They must have been lost in our rushed escape. I had failed in so many ways tonight, not the least in returning Brian's medicine to him.

"We need to get off this train before it reaches Cardiff," Lancaster said, getting up to pull on the train car door. It slid open to reveal the brightening countryside.

"We should jump as soon as it slows down into the station," I suggested, looking out at the countryside dotted with farms.

"That seems to be imminent. We're slowing down already," he replied, glancing at Nerissa.

"I'll go first," I said. "If I know Nerissa, she'll be right behind me, but if she doesn't ..."

"I'll get her out," Lancaster promised. I squeezed his hand in thanks. I was relatively sure she'd leap after me, but in case she didn't, I didn't want to leave my dog to the mercies of whoever was waiting for us at the Cardiff station.

I waited until the ground stopped whirring past me at an unseeable speed and leapt, hitting the ground hard and rolling immediately to try to distribute my re-entry. Nerissa made a much better landing a few feet in front of me, racing to my side with a look on her face like, "Next time, warn me, would you?" I pushed myself upright, feeling the bruises that would pattern my body within hours, and watched Lancaster land in much the same way as I did. Before I could do more than help him up, he and Nerissa turned to look ahead of us, where the train was pulling into Cardiff. The police had found us and were running our way from the station where they had been positioned. This was not going to be a clean getaway by any means.

Lancaster led the way, his stride outpacing mine, Nerissa fully able to overtake him, but choosing to run at my side. Lancaster might have been calling for me to keep up as he ran, but Nerissa suddenly stopped mid-sprint, her nose pointed at the forest to our right.

"Lancaster," I yelled, pulling at her collar. "Wait!"

Nerissa took off at full speed in the direction of the woodland and I had no choice but to follow her, calling her name the whole way. If she was after a rabbit … No! From the density of the wood I saw a horse emerge carrying the elegant figure of a woman. She rode out just far enough that I could see her and then expertly backed up so that she was again hidden by the distinctive birch trees. I laughed aloud as Nerissa made the edge of the trees, panting, waiting for me to catch up. My grandmother had arrived.

In a trice, we were all on horseback, my grandmother leading the way through the forest, her loyal body man, Jenkins, bringing up the rear, Nerissa running at my side. About fifteen minutes into this run we made it to an old dusty Vauxhall 30 parked behind a barn and then we were back on the road, Lancaster in the passenger seat next to Jenkins and my grandmother holding my hand in the backseat as Nerissa lapped at a bowl of water, having had the hardest escape but for the horses.

"Oh, my dear, what have you gotten yourself into this time?" were Irene Adler's first words to me. She said them aloud while writing in a notebook on the seat.

"Honestly, I have no idea," I replied, covering her hand to indicate that she didn't need to do that anymore.

"Your speech …!"

"I know. I can hear you again, and for now, you can understand me, though that basic skill seems to come and go to be honest," I said, glancing at the front seat where I could see Jenkins and Lancaster were eyeing each other distrustfully. My grandmother meanwhile pulled me close and I sank into her arms, enjoying the feeling of safety and sharing the responsibility of the situation. We weren't alone in this anymore.

"I hardly need ask how you knew where to find us," I said. "Did Brian tell you the Yard knew we were on a Cardiff train?"

She released my hands, her mouth compressing into a thin line that made it harder to read her lips. "We will discuss Constable Dawes soon, but for now, I have other sources at the Yard who alerted me to the ridiculous plans to apprehend you. I knew better than to think you would be fool enough to roll right into their hands on a train, so I picked my spot where I thought you would make a hasty exit. I was about a mile off, it turns out; you should have jumped when you saw the safety of the trees."

I don't think I'd ever heard my grandmother refer to Brian with such anger in her eyes.

"M'lady," Jenkins said, turning to face us from the driver's seat. "You said you wanted to get out with the young miss here."

"Yes," my grandmother agreed, her eyes on the waterfront where two burly men approached the car. "You will meet us tonight?"

Lancaster had put his hand on the passenger door handle, but Jenkins said something I couldn't catch and he withdrew it. "We will," Jenkins answered, turning to face me so I could see his answer. "And we'll take care of Nerissa, don't you worry."

CHAPTER 22

I FOLLOWED MY GRANDMOTHER out of the car, giving Nerissa a pat and telling her to stay put in the back. She seemed to understand that I was in good hands and that she needed to watch out for Lancaster because she climbed into the front seat between the two men. The car drove off and I turned to see my grandmother hand some money to one of the burly men as they led us to a small boat and started rowing us across the water. The port of Cardiff had once been a bustling one, but the coal industry had moved its trade routes after the Great War and we were one of only a few boats out on Cardiff Bay. Nonetheless, the men said nothing, but pulled up to a small white church on the opposite bank and rowed away as soon as we were on shore again.

"No one will bother us here," my grandmother said, leading me in through a back door. I recognized it as a Lutheran church, possibly as much as fifty years old if the iron window struts were original. It was empty, but in good condition and I followed the older woman into the small kitchen where a fine meal awaited us. My stomach must have made an audible sound because my grandmother bullied me up to the table and would answer no questions until I'd filled a plate and made a start. The strawberries were bright red and sweet, the warm loaf of bread I recognized from my favourite bakery on Lidwell Street with the toasted sesame seeds, and the cheese tray was as diverse in flavour as it was colourful. There was even a tiny pot of homemade royal jelly made for the queen bee of a hive. I had missed real food on my escapades.

"I will not be staying," she said finally, sipping at a glass of wine she had poured while I ate. She was wearing less makeup than usual, even for country life, and, looking at her boots, I noted the distinctive ash around the heels. I watched her use her pinky finger to tap a tiny amount of royal jelly at the corners of her eyes before she continued. "I must make an appearance in London to maintain this charade, but first we will take you to a safe house in Merthyr Tydfil. The city councillor there owes me a favour and will not betray us. Meanwhile, I have three lawyers on retainer working on your case in London."

"My case?" I asked, nearly choking on my bite of cheese. "What case? Grandmother, you must know that I have nothing to do with the bodies at Paddington station."

"Of course not," she said, shaking her head at me, making it harder to read her lips. "But that odious man, Kell, cannot be dissuaded that you are involved with the bombing, neither by bribe, threat, nor truth. He's been at three of my homes and he only released your friend Lord Beanstine yesterday morning after questioning the poor man overnight. Something about financing a weapons deal or something ridiculous like that. And I'm sorry to say that some government men have been picking through your Baker Street apartment looking for God knows what since you escaped into the Thames. The sooner we can throw them onto a new scent, the sooner you can come home." She handed me a change of clothing as she spoke and I thankfully started pulling on the tweed pants, a blue sweater, and a vest. All three were new and of course, fit perfectly. I folded my old clothes into a bundle and shoved them into my satchel along with the new underclothes she had provided.

"Digby killed the constable at Paddington and then himself, poor man. The forensics will be clear at least on that," I said, changing my socks and then putting my worn boots back on. "His daughter, Ilsa, is a whole other kettle of fish. I still think she's involved in the bombing, though her death would seem to indicate that she at least had an accomplice."

"Not to put too fine a point on it dear, but the dead are not as useful to us as a live suspect," she answered, lighting her tiny ceramic pipe. "Surely you have one."

I opened my mouth and closed it. I had so little evidence on the queen's lady-in-waiting that even mentioning her felt ridiculous and O'Duffy was just a convenient suspect with all the right …

"Wait, Grandmother, where is Lancaster?"

"Who?"

I got up from the table, my appetite gone. "Where has Jenkins taken him?"

"Portia …," my grandmother said, a warning in the tone of her voice and just as clear in her eyes.

"You mean to use him as a scapegoat," I whispered, anger displacing the warmth of feeling safe. I grabbed the tweed hat that completed the outfit and was out the back door before she could stop me, but the men and the rowboat were long gone. I couldn't see a car, boat, or person in sight of the church, and of course that was by design. Irene Adler had isolated me so that I couldn't halt her plan. She might be planning to keep me isolated out here, but she wouldn't leave us unguarded. If by some miracle the police found us, she would have an escape. She always did.

She hadn't followed me outside at all, patiently waiting for me to come to the right conclusion that I had no choice but to allow

Lancaster to take the fall for crimes neither of us had committed. I closed my eyes against the wind, smelling the rain that was about to douse the countryside and something else. Cheap tobacco. We weren't alone. I opened my eyes, scanning the docks.

"The bread was too fresh," I said into the wind, looking for an innocuous boat garage. I sprinted at the one closest to me and saw the trail of smoke coming up from behind it and the giggling sound of a woman he was spending his time with. I opened the door to the boat garage and found what I was looking for — an older model Ariel Red Hunter motorcycle with a generous side satchel for deliveries and a small silver key still in the ignition. I ran my hands over the controls, which weren't exactly like the ones on the motorcycle Brian sometimes borrowed from the Yard, but were similar. I'd ridden on the back a few times and had tried my hand at driving it once, finding the weight of the machine the biggest deterrent to comfort.

I carefully walked the motorcycle out of the boat garage so as not to alert its owner and only started the machine up when I gained the main road. I glanced back at the church where I thought I could see the door opening. Perhaps my grandmother had come out to mollify my concerns, but she was about to be sorely disappointed. That said, I knew she would grudgingly cover the cost of this motorcycle with its owner rather than allow it to be reported stolen. I turned my face back to the wind, instinctively driving towards London, which would be a three-hour ride north and then east. But Jenkins was coming back for Adler ... she had told him so in the car and she had said herself that she needed to return to London to maintain her charade of not being in league with me (which at this point she would not be lying about). That meant Jenkins was going to dump Lancaster somewhere closer than London. Sherlock's maps had never tracked out this far so

I didn't know where the nearest police station was, but surely it would be closer to the town. I took St. Mary Street, looking for a sign to the nearest constabulary when I noticed a pair of teenagers digging through a rubbish bin in an alley, throwing half-eaten fruit over their shoulders. Instead of hightailing it when I slowed down next to them, they turned with snarls on their faces. The older of the pair had a makeshift cudgel at his belt, which he put his hand on when I took my foot off the pedal.

"I can tell you where your mates hid last night's haul if you can direct me to the police station," I said, looking to the older one. "Or you can try to rob me, find I have no money on me, and be no closer to finding your stolen booty."

The younger boy's mouth dropped open and he looked wide-eyed at his compatriot whose snarl changed slowly to an assessing smile.

"What stolen booty?" he asked, crossing his arms in a challenge.

"You're not hungry, or you wouldn't be throwing away perfectly edible food — I know that from personal experience. No, you're looking for something you lost. Not sure what it is, but I'm guessing more than you could carry away last night when you robbed whomever you robbed against this wall. The scuffle is obvious in the way this dirt has been kicked around and there's an eye tooth over there that I'm guessing your victim lost in the fight since you both have all your front teeth. Did the police surprise you? Is that why you dropped whatever you took?"

The way they glanced at each other confirmed my guess.

I nodded. "Well, whomever you worked with on this ill-advised caper hid what you dropped with the intention of coming back here by themselves to re-acquire it. Would you like to know where it is?"

They made their decision quickly, describing the two police stations in the vicinity, and I in turn advised them to look for the stolen goods on the second-floor balcony above us. The metal stairs had been let down sometime yesterday, from the condition of the mud on the struts, and left down, which meant someone had gone up and come back down (rather than climb up and open a window to perhaps gain entry to a locked apartment). Chances are the stolen goods were hidden up there rather than down here.

I climbed back on the motorcycle and headed in the direction of the police station that was further away. If Jenkins had dropped Lancaster at the first station, it wouldn't take him this long to get back to the church. I pulled up far enough away from the building that I could hide the motorcycle in an alleyway and made my way across the street from the station, putting my foot up on the railing of a storefront to pretend to be tying my bootlace.

Nothing looked amiss from the outside — no consolidation of police cars indicating that the Yard had been called in, or at least if they had, they were still on the road from London. How would I get him out? How would I even ascertain that he had been brought here? I watched a skeevy-looking man exit the station on his own, holding a cigarette up to his nose as he came down the stairs, enjoying the smell. He turned left and disappeared into a pub a half a block away. That was my way in.

Fifteen minutes later I was wearing his clothes, my new tweed outfit tucked into my now bulging satchel and tucked under my borrowed shirt to act as a belly. I rubbed dirt on my cheeks to simulate a shadow of a beard, pulled his hat low over my eyes, and, my heart thundering in my chest, made my way up the stairs and into the station.

A constable stood just inside the front door replacing posters and information on a corkboard, and seeing myself in black and white, I fought the urge to turn around the way I had come; that would surely look more suspicious than continuing my entry. He wasn't paying attention to me anyway. He kept stealing glances at the woman manning the front desk. The object of his attentions was a woman with rigorously dyed and styled blonde hair. No ring on her finger and a blouse that left little to the imagination, all of which gave me my next idea.

"Evenin' doll," I said, in what I hoped was a reasonable impression of a male voice. "I'm here to get the dinner orders for the prisoners."

She barely glanced up at me, her gaze focused on a well-worn book. I took a chance and reached out, raising her chin so that she was looking at me. "Whaddyasay, gorgeous?"

She blushed at my attentions, glancing around to see if we were alone, and I removed my hand, giving her one of Lancaster's looks this time, that flirty non-dangerous half-smile. I had no idea it would work, but she giggled nervously and said, "Sure, we only got one, but you know where the cells are?"

"I do," I said with a tap of my hat. "Now, don't you go anywhere."

She giggled again and I walked down the only hallway that led away from the upper offices, down some stairs to find the jail area. In the farthest corner of the room sat a man I recognized. He was on his tiptoes, both hands grasped on the iron bars covering the tiny window of his cell.

"Lancaster," I whispered, nearing his cell.

He turned and did a double take, "What in God's name are you doing here?"

I carefully pulled a couple of hairpins out from under my

borrowed hat, handing them to him through the bars. "Get ready to escape, I'm going to cause a disturbance."

He grasped my hand on the bar. "You shouldn't have come back for me."

"My grandmother isn't a bad person," I said. "Well, she is a selfish person, but she's got my best interests at heart. Honestly."

"I find that easy to believe," he said, his hand warm on mine. "Jenkins seemed like a decent fellow who was truly sorry for being put in the position to trade me for your freedom."

"I half expected to find one of you bruised into unconsciousness," I admitted, looking at his face and fists for any sign of a fight. Jenkins was, after all, a former boxer of some renown, and could hold his own against a man half his age.

"I would never strike a legend like Bruiser Jenkins. My dad used to take me to his fights!" Lancaster said, managing to look slightly shocked at the suggestion. "But the truth is, I think your grandmother might have the right of it. If I am taken into custody with the Yard, the pressure will let up on you, allowing you the freedom to actually find this bomber."

"If it were the Yard who were coming for you, you'd be under guard, even here in your cell," I replied, letting go of his hands. "But Kell, as you said, keeps his cards close to the chest and has told them nothing about your alleged crimes except to lock you up. Be ready to make a quick exit."

I ran back up the stairs and slowed down as I walked down the hallway, winking at the woman behind the desk. "Meet me outside for a minute, won't you?"

Her mouth dropped open, but I turned away, trying to be mysterious, and sauntered out the door in my best imitation of my ex-boyfriend's cursed confidence. Gavin had a way of making every female in a space pay attention to him when he wanted the attention. I believe (after months of study) that it was all in his aura of confidence.

The constable who had been at the corkboard was now outside, smoking with a sergeant. Definitely not the actions of a station at high alert. Right on schedule, smoke started to rise out of the pub where I had changed into my disguise and I slapped a look of horror on my face and pointed at it.

"I will call the fire department," I assured the two police officers. "I was in that pub for lunch and two teenage boys tried to accost me as I left."

Knowing of the previous night's criminality gave me the advantage and I described the boys so well that the sergeant actually clapped me on the back as they sprinted off towards the pub to capture the teenagers who had been reported last night. The woman I was waiting for came out the door at exactly that time and I grasped her hand, pulling her into the alleyway behind the station. She immediately pressed me against the wall, whispering something breathy and urgent in my ear. She pressed kisses against my neck and I had to step back to tell her that I was delivering a message on behalf of the officer who had been standing at the corkboard.

"Larry?" she said, her colour high, her confusion apparent.

"Yes, Larry," I agreed, holding her at bay. "He couldn't stop talking about you. How beautiful you are, how irresistible, how he's been too shy to make the first move."

She stopped trying to pull me close, her eyes wide. "I've known Larry since grade school. He's never said a word."

"I think you should talk to Larry, maybe invite him for a drink, but don't tell him I told you any of this. He's a gentleman after all," I said, starting to run out of ideas as to how far I could extend this façade when I finally saw Lancaster steal out of the building.

"Fire!" I yelled, as if suddenly realizing the pub was alight, turning my would-be lover towards the danger. She covered her mouth with her hands in surprise, but I bustled her towards her home, assuring her that I would tell Larry that I had sent her to safety. I ran after Lancaster, catching up with him two blocks away, and leading him to the motorcycle. I had negotiated a tenner for the distraction and the disguise from the skeevy man, but I hoped that he didn't actually burn the place down.

Lancaster got on the back of the motorcycle without an argument and we were London-bound once more.

CHAPTER 23

"I THINK WE NEED to focus on the bombs," I said, taking a bite of the sandwich we were sharing before handing it back to Lancaster.

We were taking a circuitous route back to London, stopping in small villages along the way for breaks and for food. I had dashed into the village on foot and still in disguise to secure lunch and as many newspapers as I could carry. Now we were eating in an obliging field, the motorcycle hidden behind bales of hay. It would take us a full day to get back to the city, but we were less likely to be identified and recaptured this way.

Lancaster took a bite as well before answering, he not having had the benefit of a delicious but delay-filled meal with my grandmother and therefore ravenous. I pushed the sandwich back his way upon remembering that, eating the chips beside it instead.

"We don't have it anymore," he said. "But Kell identified it as Russian-made and I see no reason why he would lie to us about that. How does that help us?"

"Whoever is deploying the bombs is not an expert in bomb-craft, they simply have access to these old bombs," I said, getting up to pace as I often did when my mind was whirring. "Who would have access to Russian-made bombs from the Great War? Other than Box 850, of course."

"Of course," he said with a pained grin. "Former gunnery sergeants, possibly. Anyone in the military who had access to British and European military arsenals. A long list in other words."

"But the lack of expertise," I repeated. "Those mines that were strung up in the basement of The Trifle were very inexpertly done. The fact that we could disarm them by unhooking wires is laughable. There should have been trick wires and back-up systems that would be triggered by our interference."

He shrugged. "They did manage to kill someone, Portia, so they weren't entirely amateur."

"Unless they never meant to kill anyone," I said, still pacing as he finished the sandwich and reached for his beer. "If Ilsa was involved, how would she have gotten her hands on military-grade bombs?"

"A military man?" Lancaster answered after a moment's thought.

"A man she was sleeping with perhaps," I agreed. "Someone who would let down their guard enough to allow her to gain access to an arsenal."

"But why would she … Portia, we're round back to the same problem," Lancaster said. "She has no motive. Blowing up her father in his train is an extreme way to get rid of someone who you think left you at an orphanage. Surely there were easier ways to be rid of Digby. A gun for example. Like the one that killed Ilsa."

I nodded. "We keep getting caught up in the motive and I think the problem is that there might be two motives, which is confusing our suspect pool."

"What?"

"What if someone is using the bombs to kill and someone else is using them to terrify the population — taking advantage of the bombs that have gone off to create more of a panic about them?" I said.

"Without coordinating with each other?" Lancaster asked, his mouth scrunching up a bit and betraying his doubt.

"I don't know," I said with a frustrated sigh. "It's just a theory. When a single motive doesn't solidify, sometimes it's because different crimes are coalescing and making it seem like one crime rather than two. And I keep trying to link this back to the stockpiling of weapons, but I find it hard to believe that the British government is buying old Russian bombs and then losing them to a bomber who is planting them all over London. It's ridiculous."

Lancaster shook his head. "That is ridiculous. If our government is actually stockpiling weapons, which I'm not saying they are, they would be new and kept under guard day and night or there would be no point to the whole endeavour. My gut is telling me this bomber is an outside entity trying to destabilize our country. The only connection might be that they are trying to dissuade other governments from supplying us with weapons by making us look unstable and out of control. Look at the targets — Downing Street? Our transportation system? The War Office?"

"And my college?" I replied.

"That one pointed to you," Lancaster said. "Which could be part of the same motive. Upon realizing that you were a suspect because of your presence at the first crime scene, the bomber did some research, realized you were a student at King's College, and planted a bomb on campus so that more suspicion would fall upon you, allowing them to continue their work."

"If that were true, they would surely have halted once I was reported to have left London," I said, turning a page in *The Daily Mail* to where my disappearance was reported in a short column. Mrs. Dawes was described in the column as "rather hysterical at all the attention" and too busy to speculate as to my involvement. I grit my teeth against the damage this case was doing to my friends and my hard-won reputation as a consulting detective.

"Another bomb placed outside Buckingham Palace," Lancaster quoted from another newspaper. "At least this one was proved to be a hoax."

"I wonder how long it took them to check the whole palace and comfortably declare it a hoax?" I said, closing *The Daily Mail* and opening *The Lady* to scan for a message from Annie. I found my message to her right away, and a few ads down, I found hers.

I decoded it quickly, "Beans safe. No sign of Whitt. Flat watched. No one home."

I hadn't been looking at Lancaster's face, so I missed what he said, but he stood up, hearing something I did not, obviously. I shook the crumbs off my lap and we got on the road again, this time with Lancaster driving and my arms around his waist. Of course, this reminded me of my rides with Brian and I allowed myself a moment to dwell on the man I love. The clues reported by Annie, Michaels, and my grandmother added to my own brief observations since the accident laid out a few possible scenarios. Up until now I had been able to excuse his lack of engagement in my situation as one I had caused by pushing him away when I was getting used to the loss of my abilities. But the fact that he had not been in contact with Annie or Adler, that Baker Street was all but abandoned … and that he was not quoted in that article defending me, told me that either he was also on the run, he had washed his hands of me, or he had developed an addiction to the drugs that took away his pain. If he were under arrest or on the run, Annie would have found a way to communicate that, and my grandmother would not be so angry at him. If he were at his wits' end and leaving me to fix my own problems, then why abandon Baker Street? And why, as Beans had reported, abandon Scotland Yard and the only job he had ever wanted? Mrs. Dawes was retired and had never in my memory risen to the level of panic described in that column, even when her son was endangered by his job or the townhouse was under siege by the press. The only thing that could push her to hysteria (if the reporter was not exaggerating) was worry for her son.

I pressed my face against Lancaster's back. I knew my next ad in *The Lady* would have to ask for Sherlock Holmes' help. After all, who better to help an addict but a recovering one?

CHAPTER 24

WE STOLE BACK INTO London sometime after midnight. I hated to give up the motorcycle, but it was a rarity and could therefore cause people to notice us — the opposite of what we needed to do. We pulled up in an alleyway off Skeffington Street and dismounted, stretching our tired bodies. I pulled an envelope out of my satchel and popped in the motorcycle key. I wrote the address to the bakery on the envelope and this cross-street as well. Hopefully, by the time they got the key, the motorcycle would still be here.

"I still don't like the idea of splitting up," Lancaster said, leading the way down to the waterfront. "But you're right that it will be hard enough for me to get into the Royal Arsenal."

"I have other avenues to pursue," I assured him. "But the most important element is our meeting place so that we can regroup with our data."

"The Wool and Weaver is exactly the pub you're looking for," he assured me, reaching for my cold hand. "Remember to tell the bartender that you're visiting your pregnant sister. He knows where to take you. And he can be trusted. We worked together in the war."

"Like Major Collins?" I asked.

"Yes and no," Lancaster replied, leaning in close. "Are you sure you won't just head straight to the pub?"

"Are you sure you don't want to tell me about Heddy Collins?"

"I promise I will tell you everything about the Collinses as soon as you can explain their connection to this and not before," he replied.

I felt his breath on my face and nodded. "I will see you tomorrow night. Be safe."

I kissed him once, on the edge of his mouth, and then again. And then we were kissing like we hadn't seen each other in months. He tasted like that odd combination of bubble gum and Morlands — not unpleasant, but distracting. We broke it off at the same time and I turned away immediately, heart hammering, walking in the opposite direction of the Royal Arsenal, putting as much distance between me and that temptation as I could.

It took me nearly two hours to navigate my way to my destination, switching between short hops in cabs and walking through alleys I recognized only by name from Holmes' map. I dropped off the envelope with the key and my ads — one for *The Lady* and one for *The Sunday Times* where I hoped my grandfather would find it — at a post box along the way, glancing over my shoulder with a paranoia I had never felt before. Finally, I made it to Stepney Green and knocked discreetly on the door to the shop where I had been welcomed a week ago.

Once, twice, thrice I knocked, but no one answered, so I took a chance, turning the handle and finding it unlocked.

"You!" said the young boy named Lin, who had pulled me from the street to meet his aunt. He lowered his cricket bat and called out something to his aunt, who came out from behind her counter carrying a flat-bottomed pan.

"I am so sorry to bother you so late," I said, my hands raised in case they still thought I was a threat. "But I need your help."

The aunt stepped forward and clapped me on the back, speaking far too fast for me to understand even if she had been speaking in English, but pointing at me with a triumphant look in her eyes. I shushed her as best as I could, letting her lead me further into her shop.

"You can talk," Lin said, wiping the sleep from his eyes,

"I can," I said, as Lin's aunt examined me again. "But I still need you to translate for your aunt."

"You could have waited to tell us in the morning," Lin said, his grumpiness evident as he took a seat at the counter.

"I couldn't, actually," I said, gently grasping the aunt's hands and removing them from my face. "My friend is in trouble and I have a feeling you can help me find him."

Lin's aunt said something that Lin translated. "She wants to know if you stopped taking those pills."

"Why … Yes, I did, though not on purpose," I replied.

She nodded as soon she heard my "yes," speaking quickly to Lin.

"She says she knew the pills were causing the problem," Lin said.

I frowned because that was ridiculous, wasn't it? Except it wasn't. It was a possible explanation for a problem doctors hadn't been able to explain. This was a clue I hadn't been searching for in a case I thought I'd solved. I glanced at the counter where I had last seen the scrapbook Gavin had left behind.

"She wants me to go back to bed," Lin interrupted my thoughts. "You said you need help?"

I followed Aunt Chen out a back door to her shop about ten minutes later. She had sent Lin packing off to bed. We would have to communicate with her limited English.

Through the haze of smoke and dulled pain I thought I saw Portia Adams walking towards me, but that was impossible. She was counties away with her new lover doing God knows what.

I saw him right away, at the back of the second drug den Aunt Chen led me to. I walked around men in various states of stupor, leaving Chen to speak to the "helpers" who tried to get in my way.

"Brian," I said to the man I love, the man I barely recognized, his long body twisted and bent into a fetal position, his damaged hand hanging off the filthy cot like it wasn't even a part of him anymore. "I'm here. I'm back."

CHAPTER 25

I HAD NO CHOICE but to take Chen up on her offer to stay the night above her shop. We couldn't go back to Baker Street together and I was not letting Brian out of my sight again. She helped me manoeuvre Brian into the guest bed where we stripped him down to his skivvies, which he didn't resist at all, as malleable as a sleepy toddler. She left the room with the bundle of clothes, shaking her head at me as she closed the door.

"I thought the opium dens had all been closed down by the Yard in my grandfather's time," I said, pulling the worn cotton sheet up to his chest and sitting down on the edge of the bed, being careful of his injured hand, which we had left in its grimy glove.

He mumbled something I couldn't decipher and I reached out to turn his lips my way, but he flinched. I swallowed down my bile and stood. "I can speak now, Brian, and my hearing is vastly improved but I'm going to need you to speak up. I can also get you a pencil and a pad if you'd prefer ..."

He pushed himself into a shaky sitting position to look me in the eye. "I have nothing to say," he bit out, enunciating clearly, and then he rolled onto his side away from me, his arm extended in the same way it had been before.

"The Hell you don't," I hissed back.

He turned back, his eyes wide at my outburst.

"You have dropped everything in favour of your pain," I said, unable to hold back my fury. "Your family, your friends, and your job. All of it so you can wallow in misery like a … I don't even know what."

He threw himself out of the bed to answer, nearly tipping over with the effort. "I dropped everything? Who pushed me away at every opportunity? Who left me to explain your absence to your grandmother, the police … Who ran off with a fancy new man we know nothing about?"

"Are you kidding me? We were on the run — pursued by Box 850 and the Yard …"

Brian bent over at the waist, sweating at the effort of this confrontation. Then his head came up with a look of horror and, covering his mouth, he bolted to the window, yanking it open to puke down the back of Chen's building.

My anger lowered to simmer at this abject demonstration of his suffering and I walked over, my hand hovering over his back as he heaved. Not touching, because I didn't want to surprise him into hurting his hand, which, even now, he was holding away from his body. His ribs were far too visible through his skin; his back sported bed sores that spoke of how much time he spent on it. I forced my mind away from the other clues his body fed me: the scent of lilacs, perhaps from one of the helpers at the den; the bruises on his shoulder where he had fallen down cement stairs, landing badly, in an effort to spare his wounded hand. My eyes focused on his hand as he fought to catch his breath. The glove was grimy but I didn't recognize it and on closer examination, it was silk, and bespoke, if the sewing was to be believed.

"You," he pointed at me with his good hand between rasping breaths, "have no right to judge me."

"I am as damaged as you are," I retorted, my ire cooling to a dangerous level. "I've spent most of my recovery with disabilities you can't even imagine, running from place to place with people I cannot trust, all while having my reputation torn to shreds in my absence."

"I am in a pain you cannot imagine," he said, holding up his damaged hand like it was a filthy rat he'd found in his kitchen. "The pills and the opium are all that are keeping me alive."

He was still getting the pills? How was he affording them?

He wiped the sweat from his brow, leaning back against the windowsill. "Where are we, anyway?"

"A friend's house," I replied, trying to get a better look at his silken glove. There was a stitched emblem at the wrist that looked a little like a lion. "We can't stay long. I wouldn't want to risk involving her in this trouble, but we should be safe for tonight."

Reminding me of my refrain to Lancaster, Brian said, "Well, you can go anytime. I'm sure I can find my way home all on my own."

"Really? When was the last time you were home? If your trousers were any indication, they haven't been pressed in at least a week and your mother wouldn't be able to watch you walk out the door like that," I said. "She's terrified, by the way. I could tell that from a single line in a newspaper article."

He dropped his eyes from mine and I took the opportunity to move a little closer. "Brian, I am so sorry. I am as guilty of focusing on my own pain as I just accused you."

When he said nothing, I moved even closer so I could feel the warmth of his body, aching to be held. "I'm here to support you in your recovery. As long as it takes. Whatever it takes."

"Won't you need to run off and solve this bombing with your new partner?" he said, petulance hovering around the edges of the question in the quiver of his bottom lip.

I slid my arms around him. "I can't solve this without you and we can't get back to Baker Street until we clear my name and find the bomber. Will you help me?"

He bent his head and rested his clammy forehead against mine. "I'm so tired of this pain, Portia. I can't sleep. I can't think."

"I know," I whispered.

That night was the worst I've had since holding my mother as she succumbed to her cancer. Brian was at turns lucid and able to talk about his trauma and at other times so sick that his chest ached from the heaving. I kept him hydrated, washed him down with cool cloths, and warmed him back up when he shook from the cold. It took only a few hours for him to beg for his pills and then by morning he was demanding them, threatening to call the Yard and turn me in if I didn't feed his addiction.

Chen found me sitting outside the bathroom waiting for him to wash his face and gave me a cup of hot tea. She pointed at a second cup and at the bathroom door, indicating this was for Brian. Then she showed me a small sachet of tea and pointed to his cup again.

"I understand," I said, nodding wearily. "I will make sure he drinks it. And I promise, we will leave as soon as he is able to walk."

Lin joined us then, freshly washed for school, his arms full of clothes. "These were my uncle's — the pants might be a bit short on your friend, but they're clean."

"Thank you, Lin," I said. "And please thank your uncle when he gets back. I will wash them and return them as soon as I can."

Lin glanced at his aunt before answering. "My uncle died many years ago. You can keep them."

I opened my mouth to disagree, but saw the alarm on Chen's face and changed my mind, nodding instead, and watching Lin disappear down the stairs that would lead down to the store.

"You don't want him to know that your husband left," I said, once I was sure enough time had passed for the child to have left the building.

"How?" Chen asked.

"You keep these clothes in a cedar chest," I said, holding them up to my nose. "You could be saving them for Lin, but they are quite formal and old-fashioned and he's wearing much newer clothes, as are you. I suspect they are your husband's wedding clothes."

Chen nodded slowly.

"You saved his clothes, but sold his ring?" I asked, turning the shirt her way to show the slight indentation of a ring that had lain between the clothes, wrapped in wax paper for years. The wax paper had left behind slight traces as well, degrading over time. "That sounds like an angry response. If he'd died, you would have kept the ring, but if he'd left you for another woman …"

Chen's chin hardened and I knew I'd struck close to home. I reached out. "Thank you for these. I can dispose of them once Brian is done with them and you need never think of them again."

Brian coughed from inside the bathroom and the water started running again.

"Or is this like Gavin's scrapbook?" I mused aloud. "Do you keep these clothes as a ward against his return?"

"No, he not come back," Chen assured me, and then walked back to her room, her steps a little slower at the memories I had surfaced.

Brian opened the door, stopping me from pursuing her.

"I think I have thrown up or in other less pleasant ways, expelled, the entire contents of my body down to my bones," he announced in a shaky voice.

I handed him the tea Chen had delivered. "Then drink this before we get on our way. You should have plenty of room."

CHAPTER 26

TAKING A RICKSHAW OUT of Stepney Green might be considered a dangerously public way to travel, but Brian was barely able to walk down the back stairs, never mind negotiate his way onto a train platform. I worried that the walk through Chen's shop would be a dangerous one and I could see that Brian's eyes were everywhere, looking for something to fight his pain. But Chen, understanding her patient better than either of us, had covered her shelves with curtains so that neither a pill nor a plant was visible. Though he promised to master his emotions as best he could, his pain was palpable in how carefully he walked and the tears in his eyes every time we went over a bump in the road. I did my best to cushion him, but he seemed to be regaining some of his natural stubbornness, attempting to hold himself upright between bouts of heaving out the side of the rickshaw. I tipped very generously when we finally alighted from our transportation, hoping that the young bicyclist who had carried us here would not find himself questioned anytime soon.

"Where are we?" Brian said, leaning heavily against a brick wall.

"That pub over there is where we're meeting Lancaster," I said, pointing at The Wool and Weaver. It was closed because it was far too early for patrons, but I wanted the opportunity to scope the place out before the spy arrived. "We're going to wait for him at the fabric shop across the way."

I had been in this shop on several occasions, so I knew that the upstairs was a quiet spot that the elderly owner rarely visited — his knees were weak and made loud creaky noises when he attempted stairs. I peeked through the shop window to ascertain that no one was in yet, and then we made our way around to the back of the shop where deliveries were made. It took a few minutes, but I managed to pick the lock. I pushed Brian in, grabbed a rusty bin from the alleyway, and followed him up the stairs. He wheezed when he got to the top, but I led him over to sit at the window that overlooked the street. I handed him the rusty bin in case his stomach rebelled again and then strategically moved boxes of ribbons and yarn to hide him from sight. Once that was accomplished, I made my way to the basement of the shop (wherein I had seen the owner disappear for his cup of tea) to find a small kitchen, and boiled some water to steep Chen's tea in. Leaving the teapot in case it was missed, I filled a ceramic pot with the tea, ran the boiling pot under some water to cool it, and then carried the tea and a mug up to Brian.

He had been digging through various boxes, no doubt looking for something to alleviate his pain like a half-empty bottle of liquor, but had come up empty.

"His name is Lancaster?" Brian asked, trying to replace things in boxes.

"The man who helped me escape Box 850? That's what he says his name is," I answered, helping him to put things right.

Brian took a sip of the tea before speaking again. "You think he lied about his name?"

"Spies lie for a living," I replied, sitting down so we were shoulder-to-shoulder looking out on the street, to Brian's right so I could hear him better.

"But you trusted him enough to go on the run with him? To wait for him here?"

"We're waiting for him across the street to see that he comes alone and does not give me away," I said. "That's how much I trust him."

Brian seemed buoyed by that admission and I found myself remembering a passionate kiss in an alleyway not far from here. Trust did not trump chemistry it seemed. I pushed that guilt away, refocusing on my boyfriend's face. The stubble did nothing to detract from his features but his eyes looked sunken and the ever-present half moon bruising under them hadn't receded overnight.

"Milk delivery," he commented, causing me to glance back out the window to see the truck that had pulled up outside the pub.

"Brian, Gavin is back in London," I said, as the milk truck drove away a few bottles lighter. "I haven't seen him yet, but I saw his photo in the newspaper. Has the Yard been pursuing him?"

Brian shook his head ruefully. "I haven't been at the Yard in … I don't know. How long have you been gone?"

"Never mind," I said, not wanting to upset him again. "Can I see your glove? Where did you get it?"

He looked at his glove in surprise, as if having forgotten it was on his hand. "Why?"

"It just doesn't look like something you would wear … or buy."

"I didn't," he admitted, gingerly unwrapping the glove from his injured hand, wincing the entire time. I hated to put him through the pain, but I had a suspicion that needed to be satisfied. He finally worked the thin silk off the burned appendage and I held in the gasp that tried to escape me. The burn scars on the back of his hand were light compared to the deep scars on his palm.

I wanted to touch him so badly, but I knew that I couldn't. Instead I took the glove he extended my way and focused on it.

As I'd suspected, a monogram of a lion and a trident revealed itself once I stretched the material out.

"What is it?"

"This monogram. I've seen it before. Gavin was wearing this same icon on a pin on his jacket. In the photo I told you about."

"What?"

"He wants us to know he's back and he wants us to know he has his eyes on you," I replied, turning the glove over to see if there were any other distinguishing features. Other than the richness of the material and the fineness of the stitching, this was the only clue, but it sufficed.

Brian turned away to retch into his rusty bucket and I dug through my satchel for a handkerchief.

Brian grasped my wrist with his good hand, "Portia, it's worse than that. When I ran out of money to buy more medication, I found this glove and a note with an address on it in the hallway of our flat — on the telephone table."

"Gavin directed you to the drug den?" I asked, horrified at his level of manipulation.

"As long as I wore this glove, the drugs kept flowing, no matter how little money I had," Brian explained. "Now it seems insane that I just accepted that, no questions asked … but at the time, it was like a gift from heaven."

I handed Brian the kerchief, my mind whirring. "He drugged you. He may have been drugging you from the beginning. Brian did you notice any change in the pills you were taking? From when you left the hospital to the ones that got delivered to Baker Street with mine?"

Brian patted at his face and mouth and then said, "Now that

you mention it, yes, but I thought maybe your Dr. Watson had changed the prescription to be more cost-effective. Wasn't he involved in the pill delivery?"

"He was, but he didn't deliver them himself," I replied, understanding the level of Gavin's interference now and kicking myself that I hadn't seen it sooner. Chen had all but laid it out for me when I first met her. "I never saw who made the deliveries. It was always when we weren't home."

"He was drugging me?" Brian repeated incredulously. "Trying to get me addicted?"

"He was," I replied. "And I think he was drugging me too."

Brian's stopped rubbing at his mouth, his eyes wide.

"When I first met Chen, she wanted to examine my pills and she said I needed to stop taking them," I explained. "I think the hearing loss is damage from the accident. But my speech confusion, that may have been caused by the drugs or enhanced by them. Gavin minored in chemistry in his studies, remember, and he was an expert on poisons — it's why he was so sought-after as a coroner for the Yard. I think he took advantage of our injuries to take us out of service."

"He's up to something that he needs us sidelined to accomplish," Brian said, shaking his head, anger pushing his shock aside. "You don't think he's behind the bombings …"

"I wouldn't put anything past him at this point, but if I thought I had tenuous motives for Ilsa, I don't see anything for Gavin to gain other than creating wanton panic to distract from a more financially-motivated plot. He's here with a delegation from Austria, supposedly to negotiate between the Germans and the Brits," I said, my eyes back on the street where two people were approaching The Wool and Weaver. "But we have two more pressing questions to tackle right now."

The two people, one of whom was most assuredly the man I knew as Lancaster, approached the building from the back, and disappeared, most likely into the pub.

"I can go," I started to say.

"There's no way I'm leaving you alone with him again," Brian interrupted. "Plus, if you mean to listen in on them rather than confront them, you're going to need me. Unless your hearing is back to normal."

He slurped down the last of his tea and we made our way out of the shop the way we had come in. I left the back door unlocked in case we needed to come back in here today. The shopkeeper would be in within the hour and would probably think he had forgotten to lock up last night.

I led Brian down the block behind the shops and then we stole across the street from an angle Lancaster would not be able to see us should he be looking out the windows at the pub, and made our way back to The Wool and Weaver from the alley behind it. Like all the shops on this side of the street, this one was a three-storey, with the pub on the main level, storage or sleeping quarters on top and a short basement that could be accessed through a pair of barn doors. I dismissed the basement because of the chain and lock on them. If they were down there, I didn't have the equipment to pick that lock and they would surely hear us when we came down the stairs. I'd have to rely on Brian's ears to help us sneak up on them.

He put his hand on the doorknob to the back of the shop, but I stopped him. Something smelled wrong — literally. In addition to Lancaster's favoured cigarette brand I smelled something else I recognized.

"Shalimar," I whispered at Brian, pulling him away from the door, which swung open, extinguishing any hopes of escape.

CHAPTER 27

"PARTNERS," I REPEATED INCREDULOUSLY, my hand on Brian's back as he heaved over a sink in the pub's kitchen.

"Not by choice, believe me," Amélie wrote on her notepad, "but out of necessity."

"Then you are not with Box 850?" I pressed.

"Neither of us are," Amélie wrote before Lancaster could answer. He closed his mouth with a snap and looked away.

"What the Hell is going on?" Brian said, splashing water on his face before turning around to face us all. "If he's not a spy ..."

"He's been disavowed," I said, understanding Lancaster's actions for the first time since he struck Kell in that interrogation room. "You've been trying to get back into Box 850's good books to make up for something you did. Something that got you kicked out."

Amélie nodded vigorously, pointing at the words she had just written. "I thought he was phoning in bomb threats in order to ingratiate himself with the British Secret Intelligence Service. I knew of his interest in you from the first bombing and so I made myself available to help you with your recovery."

"But Amélie quickly figured out that neither of us were behind the bombings," Lancaster inserted, stepping forward again to speak. "And we joined forces. That's how I knew you were going to be at The Trifle. Amélie had seen your note to Annie when she dropped off the lip-reading books."

Annoyed as I was by this further evidence of intrusion, I couldn't help but feel a little better about having another intelligent mind at our side.

Brian sat down on a stool, nodding his head slowly. "Then you are with Le Premier Bureau?"

"Actually, Le Deuxième Bureau. Amélie Blaise," I read off the small wallet Amélie produced from her purse. "Which means you're assigned to foreign threats."

Amélie signed something that I took to be agreement.

"Does my cousin, Heather, know of this, or the Watsons?"

"No, I am good at my job, even you would not have discovered this about me if I didn't believe we could help each other stop this threat," Amélie wrote.

"I need to speak to Amélie alone," I said to the men in the room.

Brian looked ready to argue and then seemed to think he could use some alone time with Lancaster and agreed. I led the French woman into the bar and to the stairs that led to the second floor. I sat down, as did she, pen and paper ready.

"I wish I was able to sign with you, it would go much faster," I said, enunciating each word. "And I promise, I will rectify that hole in my education at my first opportunity, but for now, there are a few things I need to know."

"You want to know if I am really with the French service."

"No, I believe you at your word. As I said the first time I met you, you have lived in France, your clothes speak of a higher class of living than a simple sign language teacher, and it was very convenient that you were in town just when I needed you. When I see you now, I can add to those first impressions a penchant for spy tools like the small knife you have concealed in your hair barrette and the hollow heel in your left boot — what do you keep in there by the way?"

"Lock-picking tools at present, but anything I might need on a mission," she wrote. "Your hearing is so much better you can hear my hollow heel?"

"It's not perfect," I admitted. "But I didn't hear the hollowness of the heel, it's the faint scrape marks of sliding the heel off and on that you can see, here and here. It doesn't exist on your right boot at all. Amélie, I want to know what you know about Lancaster."

"Why?"

"Why?" I repeated, reading the word and not understanding. "Isn't it obvious?"

She glanced at the room we had just left. I realized I had been tensely listening for the sounds of a fist-fight coming from the other side. I forced myself to relax and trust Brian.

"Look, I will admit that Lancaster has come in handy while we were on the run, but I need to know that he's not working a long game with Box 850," I said.

"A long game?"

"I cannot fathom what it would be other than to divert me from my detective work, but who knows. Maybe they're trying to entice me into joining the service. Though truth be told, this is a terrible enticement."

"I know for a fact that his name is Ian Lancaster and he's not working for Box 850, but I cannot tell you why. He lost his standing while posted in Northern Ireland. A man died and Lancaster was held responsible. The Secret Intelligence Service disavowed him and claim he never worked for them at all. I know different because we have records of him from various incursions into France. Something the British government could not expunge."

"The man who died, was his name Major Collins?" I asked.

"Don't know. There was a spy whose code name was Trident who turned the Irish conflict almost single-handedly."

I shook my head. Tridents again. Every time I thought I had Gavin squared away, he rose up like a bad penny.

"There's something about that family," I said. "The wife and Lancaster have a history, I am sure of it. I can't imagine how Gavin might be connected, but I can't rule it out — even if it's one chance in a thousand."

"Gavin?"

"Long story."

Amélie hesitated and then flipped the notepad to write, "Trust Lancaster or don't, but in the meantime, new threats have come up in London."

I signalled for her to follow me back into the kitchens. If we were going to talk about the case, we needed all the data and Lancaster had some I needed.

I opened the kitchen door not sure what to expect, so I was pleasantly surprised to see the two men sharing a bottle of rum, sitting on two barstools. I had a moment to wonder if they had discussed me at all, but if Lancaster had spoken of our stolen kiss, Brian was doing a remarkable job of acting like he didn't care. Or maybe he was three sheets to the wind.

"Lancaster found where the bombs were taken from," Brian announced as soon as we were close enough to read lips.

"Not from the central armoury, but the whole system's up in arms because the bombs went missing from some former colonel's personal stash," Lancaster explained, turning his face towards Amélie so she could read his lips. "The man was taken in for questioning by both Kell and Scotland Yard, but he'd forgotten he even had them down in his cellars. He took them at the end of the Great War, some kind of souvenir or something, and it was his daughter who remembered them when the bombs were identified by the Yard in the papers."

"She dragged him down to the cellars to discover they were missing and then tattled on him to the police," Brian said with a shake of his head. "I'm all for civic duty, but that must have made for a cold family dinner that night."

Lancaster actually laughed at that joke, a sound I had never heard but sounded good coming from him. Brian smiled, another thing I had missed very much, and I stepped closer to him, being careful of his injured hand.

"So, the bombs were taken from the colonel, who wasn't really paying attention and has no idea when or who took them," Amélie had meanwhile written on her pad, "and they are being deployed by an amateur, according to the two of you."

"Yes. But are all the stolen bombs accounted for? We pulled eleven off the ceiling of the basement in The Trifle and one exploded at the train station and at the college," I said.

"The colonel remembers there being at least thirty," Lancaster said ruefully, stubbing out his cigarette. "And his daughter corroborates that story."

"Then there could be more than seventeen mines still out there," Brian said, reaching for the bottle again and deciding against it. Lancaster offered one of his cigarettes instead. The tobacco seemed to improve the colour in his face, which wasn't surprising as that was just another drug. At least this one was less addictive.

"Another threat was called in this morning, to Balmoral Castle,"

Amélie wrote. "The royal family aren't there, but the papers are reporting it as if it was a direct attack aimed at the king."

"The threat was called in this morning and it's already in the papers?" I asked.

Amélie nodded in response.

"We need to anticipate the next threat," Lancaster said. "We need to be there ready for this bomber to strike again."

"We have three opportunities to test theories," I agreed. "I, for one, am headed for Buckingham Palace."

CHAPTER 28

WE DISPERSED TO WHERE our respective instincts led us with the plan to regroup three days hence at The Wool and Weaver. Lancaster went back to Downing Street where he was sure another attempt would be made on the prime minister, Amélie was going to speak to the colonel and his daughter, Alisha, and then apply her skills at the pubs lining the Kilburn district, liking Éamon O'Duffy best as a suspect. That left Brian and me with Buckingham Palace, a huge piece of real estate to cover with hundreds of people inside and outside the gates. I convinced him to come with me rather than head back to the Yard with the argument that so big a target needed two able bodies, but the truth was, I didn't want to let him out of my sight for fear he would be pulled back towards his addiction.

Fortunately for our work, it was pouring buckets today in London, so tourists and even working Londoners were not hanging about outside the gates of the palace. Unfortunately, that meant that it was hard for us to do the same without calling attention to why two mad humans were staring up at the home of the royal family in a rainstorm. I snagged one of the urchins begging under a small copse of trees, handing her a coin to find Ruby and bring her this way — there was another coin in it for her if she did it right quick. She took off like a shot and we

stepped into a phone box so Brian could ring up his parents —
a phone call that was a long time coming and resulted in tears
on both ends of the conversation. They heard my voice and were
very appreciative that I'd found their boy and brought him back
to our work. Cognizant that Baker Street was still being watched
by Box 850, the Yard, and possibly Gavin, we gave no details as
to where we were or when we could be expected at the apartment. Brian hung up the phone and leaned against the glass wall
of the phone booth.

"How bad is your pain today?" I asked, purposefully looking
away from his hand that was no longer encased in the silk glove.

He took a minute to answer. "The truth is, not as bad as it was
before. I think the pain was so bad at first that I was terrified to
feel it again, so I medicated and then medicated again before
I needed to medicate. I stopped measuring my pain and just
avoided it.

"I'm ashamed to admit that I'd never felt that kind of pain
before. I couldn't think … I couldn't feel anything but the pain."
He looked at his hand, flexing it carefully, his eyes crinkling to
indicate how hard that movement was. "I can't believe I was
so easily manipulated into addiction. Even now I can feel the
siren call for its effects. I don't need it, but I do — does that make
any sense?"

"My limited experience with opium comes from the *Case of
the Wild Revelers* if you recall, with that group of students at
Exeter. But according to Watson's notes on Holmes, addiction
comes in many forms and answers many ills, from pain to
boredom," I answered, glad we could talk about this openly.
"When we get back to Baker Street, I will do more of a study
on the subject. We will conquer this too."

He nodded, pointing at two young girls running through the

rain in our direction, "Meanwhile, your Baker Street Irregulars have arrived in double-time."

We pulled the girls into the relative dryness of the call box and Ruby earned her commission in that moment. The palace was interviewing gardeners today at 1:00 p.m., inviting them in through one of the back doors. She knew this because one of her peers had overheard two barflies discussing the opportunity outside a pub three nights ago as they smoked over a dumpster. The children intended to source broken umbrellas from rubbish bins and sell them to the hopeful applicants as they stood in queue in the rain.

We hurriedly made our way to the side entrance on the agreement that we would be the first to buy an umbrella from Ruby, thereby lending credence to her enterprise. Brian and I devised our plan along the way and Ruby promised to contact Annie with the update that we were together as soon as she'd exhausted the coin purses in the queue. There were only a dozen or so people who had braved the downpour, so when the gates opened, we were all ushered in together, shivering in the outer lobby of the downstairs kitchens. I watched a trio of young butlers rush about with silverware and two young maids giggle on their way to their lunch breaks as they passed.

A starchily dressed butler escorted the first applicant out of the lobby and up the stairs, and I took a moment to introduce myself to the men standing at the door.

"Sir, may I step into the powder room?" I asked the very old man with a white beard that would rival Moses.

"Eh? I don't think so, quite out of the question," he answered, a look of surprise crossing his face at my voice.

I stepped even closer and the man actually leaned away from me, "Sir, it is a very delicate thing ... I really must insist, or I might … embarrass myself in Buckingham Palace of all places … and thereby involve you and these fine people in my humiliation. Please. I will be no trouble."

He turned three shades of red contemplating the variety of things that could mean and stammeringly directed me down the hall. I didn't look back at Brian as I left, trusting that he would get me out of any trouble I found myself in — no matter how he was suffering.

I walked directly to the room indicated, stepping in and turning on the light. I counted to twenty before I chanced opening the door again, ascertaining that the bearded man wasn't watching me, and locked it behind me with the light still on. Hopefully that would keep them at bay for as long as I needed. Plus, Brian had several distractions in mind to make them forget me entirely.

I had left my satchel with Brian just in case he needed any of my tools, so, I followed my nose until I found the room I wanted — the laundry. In a trice I was dressed as a palace maid, my hair tucked into a simple bonnet, and I was climbing the stairs carrying a bundle of folded towels, my heart in my throat.

The palace was busy with staff today, but no one questioned who I was or what I was about. I picked out a newer member of the staff — as evidenced by her anxiously bitten fingernails, unhemmed uniform, and high heels.

"Excuse me, Miss?" I whispered, pasting a look of terror on my face. I caught her attention and ducked behind a pillar. To my delight, she took the bait and came around to see what I was doing.

"What in heaven's name?"

"Please, you must help me, Miss," I blurted out, clutching at her sleeve and causing her to look around to make sure no one was looking at us. "I was to deliver these towels to a Mrs. Wilans ..."

"Ms. Wilans," the young maid corrected. "Then go on, deliver them, what matter is it to me?"

"I've gotten turned around three times looking for the right room," I whispered, hoping my performance was as good as it sounded in my head, because I had to be quick lest Brian be left alone too long. "Where am I to take them? Do you know?"

"To her rooms, I am sure," the maid said, succeeding in removing my desperate hand from her arm, and directing me. "Take the second door through that hallway, go up the stairs and all the way to the end to find Ms. Wilans' room. Go on with you! Before you get us both sacked!"

I took off at my fastest walk, cataloguing things against my will as I sped to my destination: the cook who was skimming from the kitchens, the butler having an affair with two of the maids and keeping them both in the dark.

I reached the second door through the hallway and nearly dropped my towels. Three corgis came barrelling towards me chased by none other than the young daughters of the Duke of York, Elizabeth and Margaret. They raced right by me, paying me absolutely no heed, calling after their puppies, and chased in turn by no less than two stern-looking nannies. I gave myself a moment to catch my breath and then continued on my way, climbing the stairs and keeping the towels in front of me until I'd reached the end of the hallway. I knocked on the door, hoping against hope. Once, twice, finally the older woman I'd only ever seen in the papers swung the door open, an angry look on her face. "Did you not hear me call out 'Come in' several times?"

"I wasn't sure," I admitted, truthfully. "I am so sorry, it's my first day."

"Are those for me or for the duchess?" she asked, pointing at the towels in my arms.

I closed the door behind me before I answered. "Truth be told, Ms. Wilans, the towels were the ruse to gain me entrance to you."

Wilans looked understandably taken aback, stepping to a bell pull at the edge of her bed. "His Majesty …"

"Please don't raise the alarm, I am not here for the royal family," I said, putting down the towels and raising my hands placatingly. "Though I am relieved by your first instincts to protect them. My name is Portia Adams. I'm a consulting detective from Baker Street and I think you know why I am here."

She had her hand on the fringed pull, but halted at my last words. She kept a hold of the alarm, but asked, "Why would you say that?"

"Your hands have healed," I asked instead of answering her question. "May I ask how you injured them?"

She looked surprised at the question, but answered automatically. "I reached for a pan of biscuits for my nephew before the pan was cool." She opened her palms to me so I could see the slight reddening of the skin in the straight lines that would support her explanation.

"Right, so then the bomb threats you were making against the palace were opportunistic, not terrorist," I said.

Her hands flew to her mouth, but not with surprise, I suspected, with horror that I had arrived at her motives.

"You took advantage of the threat on behalf of the royal family," I said. "Trying to turn some of the public's rage into empathy. It was the call this morning that put the possibility in my head. Why call the papers at the same time as the police unless your prime goal is the coverage of the threat rather than the threat itself?"

Whatever she said was lost to me because it was whispered behind her hands.

"I'm sorry, but my hearing is not the best and if I can't see your lips, I have no chance of understanding you at all," I said. "I'm getting better at lip-reading, but I need to see your lips to do that."

"You can't hear? You're a detective who can't hear?" she asked, stepping towards me.

"I know, implausible and I'm thankful to say, improving every day. To answer the question I think you asked earlier, I was forced to extrapolate from the evidence. You were so vociferous in your defence of the royal family, according to several press reports. And just now, I confirmed your instincts when you reacted in defence of the family you serve, rather than yourself upon learning I was not who I seemed."

"I meant no harm, I swear," she said, sitting on the edge of the bed, reaching out and folding and refolding the towels. "I saw how the police leapt to put more security in place for Their Majesties, and I thought, maybe the public could be turned towards defending them rather than protesting against them."

"But what about the distraction to those of us trying to solve this actual crime?" I said, sitting down next to her for a moment. "Or the police who are now wasting resources at Balmoral instead of focusing on the real criminal?"

She hung her head in answer, her chin nearly disappearing into her starched collar, "Will you allow me to tell Their Majesties myself? Before you call the police?"

"Sadly, I will not be turning you in," I said. "As I am the more likely person to be arrested of the two of us. No, Ms. Wilans, if you can assure me here and now that your campaign of distraction is done, then we shall never speak of it again and I shall tell no one what I know."

The older woman looked stunned for a moment and then threw her arms around me in what I'm sure was a rare moment of outward emotion.

"But I do need something from you in turn," I said as soon as she released me.

CHAPTER 29

I FOLLOWED MS. WILANS back down to the laundry where I picked up my own clothes from the shelf as she went and retrieved Brian.

"If you still want to do this, we must do it now," Wilans said to me as I tucked my clothes back into the satchel Brian was carrying.

"Do what?" Brian said.

"Yes, we do, but please, do not risk your position over this," I said. "If you leave us at an appropriate spot, we can do the rest."

She looked Brian up and down, her gaze lingering on his wounded hand, and then picked out a pair of folded clothes on a laundry shelf. "These were left behind by a thieving young butler. He will not be returning and you do not look presentable enough to go where I am taking you."

Brian flushed and took the clothes with thanks. I stepped out into the hallway with Wilans while he dressed.

"You must tell me what you meant when you said you were more likely to be arrested than I was," she said, glaring at an older maid who dared to try and cross our path. The woman backed up and went in a different direction.

"There are certain people who believe that I am in league with the bomber," I explained to Wilans. "It is one of many reasons

I must unearth the actual criminal. I can't go home until I'm cleared and Brian ..."

We both looked at the closed door and to my surprise, Wilans reached out a hand. "He's suffering, poor boy, that much is clear. My eldest brother came back from the Great War looking like that. Damaged and in so much pain he wasn't thinking straight. You must watch him carefully. My Eli, he was shot in the back fighting in Passchendaele. Never really recovered and never had a sober day since he got back."

"Is he ...?"

"Gone, poor thing," Wilans said, taking her hand off my shoulder and wrapping it around herself. "Never had a chance. If I knew then what I know now ... just watch him. For his own sake, watch him. No matter how strong he says he is or how truthful you want to believe he is. The hurt is a fang-toothed monster to be sure, but the painkillers he uses to fight against it are a treacherous beast all their own."

I nodded, a shiver running down my spine at her words. Brian opened the door and revealed the man I remembered. He had washed his face and combed down his hair, and the clothes fit him like a glove.

Wilans led the way back up the stairs and in the opposite direction of my first trip through the palace. Brian walked in step with me and I reached out to hold his good hand, squeezing it. He asked no questions, trusting me and my instincts, and this woman I had put my faith in not to turn us in to the Secret Service.

She led us into a small library with a simple wooden desk near the window that overlooked the gardens and bade us wait there.

Brian stepped straight to the desk where several newspapers were neatly folded, sifting through them. I was drawn to the bookshelves that lined this office from floor to ceiling, smiling at the shelves near the bottom where children's books could be seen, along with a primer and a pencil case. The rest of the books told a clear story about the history of the room, tomes that were passed down and rarely opened. I touched one that was less dusty than the rest, a terribly boring book by the looks of it, tracking international trade agreements since the Great War.

"Annie has left us a message," Brian said, opening *The Lady*'s advertising pages for me to see. "If I'm remembering our skip code correctly, it says that she's decided to take the next train out to Sandwell in the Black Country ... but that can't be right, can it?"

I took the paper from him and deciphered the same message.

"She came to me, I think, a week ago?" Brian rubbed his head, wincing, as if the memory were buried under something heavy.

"Her father has gone missing from the mine where he works," I said, taking pity on him. "She ... came to you for help in finding him."

Brian lost some of the colour in his face and at first I thought it was because of what I had said, but following his gaze, I realized the man we had been waiting for had entered the room.

"So sorry, I thought ... that is, I was told ...," the man said, looking behind him and then back in the room, his hand still on the doorknob.

"Yes, Your Highness," I said, dropping into a curtsey. "You are here for us."

"But you are not my brother's valet," he said, still confused. "I was told to come in here and find out why he didn't return from Fort Belvedere. He was to attend *The Rose of Persia* with us and did not arrive."

I was finding it difficult to understand the man's words as he had a pronounced stutter, something my partner understood right away.

"Your Highness, we are honoured to make your acquaintance," he said coming forward and extending his good hand. "This is Miss Portia Adams and I am Constable Dawes of Scotland Yard."

"Portia Adams," the prince said, only now coming into the room fully and closing the door behind him. "The consulting detective from Baker Street? Granddaughter to Dr. Watson of the same address?"

We shook hands each of us and the prince invited us to take our ease in the leather chairs. "But what are a constable and a detective doing in Buckingham Palace? And disguised as members of my staff? Please tell me this is not about my brother."

"No sir, I am not from Special Branch," Brian said, referring to the officers assigned to follow the Prince of Wales and his newest love interest, Wallis Simpson, around London. A detail that was not favoured amongst the metropolitan police. "Miss Adams and I are working on the bombing case and we find ourselves in the precarious position of evading the Secret Intelligence Service even as this bomber evades us."

I fought down an inappropriate smile of gratitude at this description of the situation, including himself as an equal in my troubles.

Prince Albert sat back in his chair, but seemed unsurprised by this statement, prompting me to ask, "Sir, I have but a few questions that will help us in our quest. The first is, how many Secret Intelligence Service agents are in the palace?"

"None, as far as I know," Prince Albert replied, opening up his jacket pocket to retrieve a pack of cigarettes. He lit one before continuing, the smoke calming his stuttering, making his lips a little easier to read. "But my father, the king, may know otherwise, so I advise you go through the proper channels to hear from him. I would not advise sneaking into his office the way you have today."

"No, of course not," I agreed. "But you have met with agents recently, perhaps two days ago?"

Albert looked startled and glanced at Brian, who said, "You'd better tell us how you know that, Portia, before His Royal Highness forgets he invited us to sit."

"In the papers, you were reported to be attending a play with the Duchess of York and, as you said, your brother, who missed the event," I said.

"Yes, and so I did," the prince replied.

"But if you had actually sat through the play you would have known that they had a last-minute change," I said. "Instead of *The Rose of Persia*, they put on *Tantivy Towers*. The apology from the theatre director is printed in the newspaper on your desk."

Albert gave in to a small smile. "I hadn't read the papers yet."

"Nor did you attend enough of the play to notice it was not the one you came to see," I answered. "Meaning someone pulled you out of the play near the beginning and kept you occupied for most of the show. I would hazard a guess that very few could do that, save your father or perhaps someone you trusted in the Secret Service."

"Someone at Box 850?" Brian asked, looking back and forth between us.

"Not Colonel Kell, or His Royal Highness would have already called him upon meeting us," I said. "But possibly MI5?"

Albert lit another cigarette off the burning end of the one he'd just finished, offering Brian one as well. Brian readily took one, his hand shaking slightly as it was lit.

"Someone I know from his efforts on behalf of this family and trust implicitly," the prince said finally. "Something I cannot say for the two of you, so you'll forgive me if I don't name names."

"Trident?" I asked, playing a hunch and receiving nothing back from the prince at all. Not a nod nor a denial.

"The agents are pursuing more than just me as a line of investigation; have they made progress on the next potential target?" I asked when he continued to smoke.

"They believe the palace is a target and have suggested we move to another location. You'll understand if I don't tell you where or when we will be going," he replied, taking another long drag off this cigarette.

"Of course," I replied, my mind skipping through the conceivable locations and arriving at two potentials, neither of which needed to be revealed at this meeting. "But other than the palace?"

"Downing Street has been ruled out, so the focus is on the travel hubs — the airport and the many train stations around London."

"The key goal of the terrorist being assumed to be a disruption of traffic," I nodded. "What about trade? What about the ports?"

"The ports too, as well as border crossings," the prince agreed, glancing at the book I had looked at on his bookshelf. "Our forces are spread out and reinforced by the fine men and women of the military as well."

"What are you thinking?" Brian asked me.

"If you wanted to draw attention away from your goal, spreading all the investigative minds of London like this would be effective," I said, getting up to pace, as I so often did when thinking hard.

I was walking and thinking, so I missed the exchange between the prince and Brian, but on my third pass, my partner stopped me by reaching for my hand. "Portia, His Royal Highness asks what makes you think that this is not a terrorist act by an outside government looking to disrupt the usual business of the empire?"

"Other than the fact that this is an amateur venture that has succeeded once and only by mistake?" I answered. "I don't know. Not for sure. But if it is government-funded terrorism, I think the combination of minds at MI5, SIS, and Scotland Yard are more than up to the task of hunting that down. My mind always pulls to the outsider agenda. Is there any chance these bombings are affecting our negotiations with the Germans? Or our reported efforts to stockpile weapons?"

The prince tamped out his cigarette. "Well, this has been most interesting. I must say, young lady, I read much about your grandfather's exploits with Holmes when I was a child and I'm glad to have met you and seen your mind in action. I sincerely hope you are right about this bomber and their motivations because I'd rather deal with one man than a country. I'd really rather stay here and discuss this further, but I must make some introductions on behalf of our coalition government." He stood and Brian did as well, bowing as I curtsied. "You will find your own way out I'm sure," said the prince. "And please don't take this the wrong way, but next time, I expect to meet you through official channels."

CHAPTER 30

TO OUR SURPRISE, WILANS met us outside the door holding two large mail sacks.

"Food and some more clothes that I put together from the hand-me-downs from the family," she explained, placing a bag over each of our shoulders carefully. "Don't try and turn me down, I can well see that you need the help. Also, a bottle of aspirin for you, sir."

"I wonder, Ms. Wilans, if we might keep these uniforms for a bit longer?" I asked.

She looked surprised, but agreed without question and motioned for us to follow her down the hall and out another door. Then we were back outside in the pouring rain, running for the nearest café awning in sight and looking in the windows at the empty tables where a single man in a woolly cap nursed a cup of tea. I was about to go in when Brian stopped me to say something I had been anticipating for some time.

"Well, that was a non-answer if I've ever heard one from the prince, which means for me to be at all useful to our investigation, I must go back to the Yard," he said as he looked down at his damaged hand with less anger than before. "I don't know how to ... How will I explain?"

"Tell them the truth," I advised, wishing I could go with

him, stand by his side for whatever punishment he had earned. "Michaels respects you enough to listen and he's probably been as worried about you as your own parents."

"What was that about Trident?" Brian asked. "I thought that was Major Collins' code name? Lancaster said Collins was dead."

"According to Amélie, Trident was crucial to the efforts in Northern Ireland," I said. "But who knows which spy she was referring to. Maybe that's something else you can pursue at the Yard."

"But that leaves you with …"

"Lancaster and Amélie, I know," I replied. "But I won't be alone."

His head came up at that.

"No one will look for me in the Black Country," I said. "And we aren't regrouping with the spies for another two days. Plenty of time to find Annie's father and bring her back with me to London."

"What about the bomber?" Brian asked, perhaps rightfully pointing out my more selfish motives in solving my friend's case first. "He may strike again while you are away."

"He or she may threaten it again, but I don't think we will see an actual bomb be set off," I replied. "Call it a hunch, for now. And God forbid a bomb does go off, the Yard will be there first to gather evidence and you shall have to be my eyes and ears, because if I were to show my face …"

"And … I promise, Portia, I am done medicating away my pain," he said, his jaw set and his brown eyes locked on mine unwaveringly, as if he could hypnotize me into believing his words. "I have learned my lesson. I won't let you down again."

"No, I don't believe you will," said the older man who had appeared at our side, silent to me, but even, it seemed, a surprise to my partner. Sherlock Holmes stood at the door to the café he had just exited and I walked into his open arms with a fair amount of relief.

"I know it's pointless to ask how you knew I would be here," I whispered into his ear. "But I am so glad you are."

He pulled back from me to give me a view of his lips. "Of course I'm here my dear, whenever you need me. I got in this morning and have been avoiding the crowds of London by reading as many newspapers as one could in such dreadful weather. Come, let me set you up with a bit of food before we go on. I see your hearing has returned?"

"A discernible improvement and I can communicate now that I am no longer taking Gavin's special pills," I replied, unable to keep the bitterness out of my voice as I followed him to his recently vacated table.

"Ah yes, your former beau is proving quite talented in manipulation," Holmes said, extending a hand to Brian and then using it to pull him close, to look him over closely. "And your current beau is paying for our miscalculation. I think you should take the aspirin you're carrying around in your sack. Here, down the hatch with a spot of tea. Like you, I hoped young Whitaker had learned his lesson and left his foray into crime behind, following a lucrative path of foreign affairs. Instead, he has used his good standing to come back to London as a diplomat and weave his web around the one person I cherish the most."

He slid an arm around me. "And for that, he must pay. No more allowances made for the man who once loved you, Portia. He must pay for his crimes in the light of day."

I nodded, swallowing down the lump in my throat. "But what are his crimes?"

"His present one?" Holmes said, his grey eyes on mine. "Power. Amassing as much as he can. By aiding in these negotiations, he's becoming invaluable to the men he represents and impressing the men across the table — on both sides, mind you. I believe he might even be funnelling the weapons your young journalist has been pursuing into the hands of the British government."

"From where?" I asked. "Surely the Austrians aren't going against the Germans by supplying …"

Holmes tapped out his pipe before answering. "No, I don't think the weapons are coming from the Austrians and they have nothing to do with these Russian bombs at all. I need more data to answer that question my dear."

I felt much better after a half hour with Sherlock Holmes, who asked a great many questions that led us down new routes of possibility. I changed back into my regular clothes and then when Brian went to the washroom to change into one of the new outfits Wilans had provided, I made sure my grandfather was fully apprised of Brian's situation.

"I have seen many a good man led astray by the sinister influence of the opiate," he said, putting a few coins on the table where we had been sitting. "I will not only keep an eye on him, but I will commission a few of your craftier Baker Street Irregulars to watch him as well."

"He says he has it under control," I said, rising to my boyfriend's defence despite myself. "But addiction, as you know, is defined by the fact that you are not in control. The drug is."

Sherlock Holmes nodded, his grey eyes drifting away from mine for the first time in our conversation. Watson had diagnosed his long-time partner with an addiction to cocaine, but as far as I knew, Holmes himself had never accepted the diagnosis. This reaction seemed to indicate that he still wasn't ready to label his use of the drug as an addiction. If he were still partaking of his favoured seven percent solution, I saw none of the tell-tale physical signs on him right now.

Brian exited the washroom looking very handsome in his royal hand-me-downs and the change gave him back some of his old confidence. We said our goodbyes, Brian eliciting my promise to see him two days hence, with Annie, if at all possible.

He was exiting the ornate gates, a personal guard holding an umbrella over his head as he made his way to the waiting car when he saw her. He ducked into the car and then chastened himself for his reaction. She was the one who was being hunted, not he. He instructed the driver to idle here where he could observe her in relative anonymity through the dark windows. She watched the two men (one of them the fallen constable dressed in clothes far above his station) and then she glanced back his way. He met her eyes through the window, remembering falling into their violet depths. As much as his heart missed the excitement of being with someone who matched his every need — mental and physical — he had learned to push that aside for the safety of his future. Loving Portia Adams would mean settling for second place. Beating Portia Adams would mean quite the opposite.

CHAPTER 31

THE TRAIN TO SANDWELL was uneventful as far as I knew, perhaps partially because I had changed into my simple vest and jacket and pulled the tweed hat down over my forehead so I could get a couple of hours' sleep. I woke as we were pulling into the station, to my surprise hearing the conductor. I could surmise that the announcement was about the station, but it felt like I was hearing just a little clearer, like the dulled piano sounds were a little sharper, under slightly less water.

Maybe that was just wishful thinking, but I retrieved my bags with a lighter step, moving through the crowd and onto the platform. I had decided along the way to locate the nearest ladies' hostel, because I knew Annie's finances would not allow for anything more costly. I hazarded asking about the hostel at the ticket desk, skipping the first booth, and instead waiting for the near-sighted ticket seller in case the posters with my face on them had made it as far out as this location.

"Old Nan's place is the only spot out here," the man said, squinting at me through the open window. "But I think she's full up, t'be honest — I've had a couple young ladies like yourself ask about a place to stay tonight — is there some kind a' convention or somethin'?"

I left with mysterious smile as my only answer, hailing the

sole taxi idling at the station and was knocking on the door to a house with a recently forsaken garden within a half hour.

"What?" demanded the middle-aged woman who answered the door who was surely not Old Nan. "Who're you, then?"

"I'm looking for a friend."

"Aren't we all, doll face?" she interrupted me, leaning against the doorway and looking me up and down. "Ain't no friends here for the likes of you though."

"Her name is Annie Coleson. Is she staying with you?"

"Mayhap she is," the woman replied and then yelled at someone over her shoulder. "It's not really our policy to give out that kind of information ..."

I pulled out my coin purse, anticipating that the policy was more of a monetary one than a moral one and the woman confirmed my assumptions, extending her hand, revealing a light rash on the palm. She turned to yell back at the person I suspected was the real "Nan" and then watched greedily as I counted out a few bills for the required information.

"Might be that a blonde girl going by the name of Annie's in a little bit of trouble," she said as she pocketed the bills. "Could be that you could find her at the police station on Harvills. Best take the bus at the corner into town."

"Thank you for the advice. May I extend some of my own? You may want to be kinder to your grandmother," I said, putting away my pocketbook.

"Huh?"

"The woman I presume you are yelling at in the house," I replied. "You may think that you're waiting her out until she dies and this house becomes yours, but your syphilis has advanced to the point that she may yet outlive you."

She hid her hand behind her back, so I turned away and threw back over my shoulder, "You may need her more than she needs you soon. I'd be kinder to her knowing that."

The courthouse was a converted manor house of red brick and wrought iron, chosen, I was sure, for its intimidating façade. Wearing my borrowed maid's uniform, I entered through the back entrance that led into the kitchens, passing a man who was urinating against the building. As I had hoped, my uniform wasn't much different than that of the kitchen staff here, a grey linen dress with a white apron. The biggest difference was the fanciness of the hair bonnet, so I removed that hastily and tucked it into my apron, leaning over to rub some grease on the too-white apron. I tucked my satchel and Wilans' mail bag into an open cubby in the mudroom and walked into the kitchen.

"You there," said a skinny cook with a white moustache from one corner of the kitchens. "You filling in for Marta?"

"Yes, ma'am," I answered meekly.

"Get this tea up to the judge's chambers quick now," she said, handing me a tray and bustling me out of her space. "And take care and wait outside his chambers to take it back down!"

The staff at so small a courthouse was minimal, so I passed no one as I walked up the back stairs that led into the judge's chambers. I knocked on the door, and entered, finding no one inside. I quickly placed the tray on the large desk and looked at the mess of papers on the desk, the single photo of the judge and his family, and the remnants of the last three meals he had eaten here. A quick scan made it clear that there was no logic to this display, but that was a clue in itself. A disorganized desk meant this judge didn't have a reliable assistant to help him and may indicate a docket that was overloaded — something I could use to my advantage. I opened the nearest filing cabinet and pulled out files and documents at random, spreading them over the desk and exchanging them for more current files which I placed at random in the cabinet. The corkboard behind the desk held equal promise, with the list of cases from last June and two very old posters listing local men being sought for two different crimes. I left the way I had come, taking the stairs back down to the kitchens and, ignoring the cook, who was now scolding a young boy, flipped my maid's uniform for the fanciest outfit Wilans had provided, a long skirt and white blouse with more ruffles than I had ever worn in my life. I pulled my hair into a chignon, threw my satchel over my shoulder, and walked out of the back door and in through the front doors of the courthouse, nodding at the singular bailiff standing out front.

I saw Annie well before she recognized me. She was sitting on a hard, wooden bench, looking like she hadn't slept in days.

She looked up only when I sat down next to her and I put my arm around her, all the communication that was required. She sobbed into my shoulder as I rubbed her back, not hearing anything she was mumbling. When she was spent, I handed her a kerchief and asked her to repeat what she had said.

"My father has been charged with murder, Portia," she sniffed, rubbing at her cheeks with my kerchief. "His trial is a sham, the man assigned to represent him a drunk, and the prosecutor an unapproachable monster. He will hang for this. And I haven't even been allowed to see him. The only moments I have had are in this courtroom where they won't even let me speak to him or pass him a note. And he's not even defending himself against the charges. Oh, Portia. What will we do? What will I tell my brothers?"

"We will tell them to get their toys out of their parents' room for their father will be home soon," I replied, squeezing her shoulder. "And meanwhile, I will take over your father's case this very moment."

"How?"

"Is this the drunk lawyer you spoke of?" I said in reply, noticing a disheveled man exiting the men's room and recognizing him from his outside urination activities earlier.

She nodded, so I left her there on the bench holding my satchel and approached the man.

"Sir, I need you to do something at this morning's hearing," I said, giving the man a once-over. "I'm a law student from London and I need you to introduce me as your associate and hand the case over to me. I will ask for a one-day extension to catch up on the case and you will support me in this."

The sweaty man gaped at me, running his own kerchief over his face as I spoke, as if he could just as easily erase me from his gaze.

"Your father-in-law is the judge, which surely is the only reason you have this job as a court-appointed defence," I said. "And he doesn't know that you have been stepping out on his daughter with someone from the local mining company. I only hope that the man you've been seeing isn't actually involved in this alleged murder because then you have escalated your crimes from philanderer to accessory."

He took a step back at my words, almost running into the door he had just left, giving me my last clue.

"If I were to step into that bathroom behind you, I believe I would find your lover, which is remarkable to me," I said. "That you would engage in such activity right under the nose of your father-in-law. But perhaps that is part of the thrill. Or perhaps this is your only opportunity to philander because your wife suspects you and demands an account of all your time. I care not. The cocaine on your kerchief and the ill-fitting belt tell enough of a story. Your lover is a bigger man who often attaches tools to his belt. You should exchange it back with him before he leaves for work or he will not be able to do his job. I'll wait for you out here with Miss Coleson so we can proceed with my plan."

With that, I returned to Annie's side. She was reapplying her makeup when I sat down and I asked her to do the same for me; we needed to make the right impression on the judge.

By the time the doors to the courtroom were opened, we were ready. We followed the bailiff inside to an empty courtroom where I positioned myself at the defence table and Annie sat directly behind me in the gallery. The bailiff looked like he wanted to correct me, but frowned when the lawyer sat down beside me as if I were supposed to be there.

"I will do as you say, but Billy has nothing to do with this case. He wasn't even in Sandwell when the foreman was killed, I can prove it," he mumbled at me, still sweating and now smelling of urine as well as body odour. "But I cannot leave you alone in this courtroom without an excuse. My … The judge will not have it."

"Your obvious illness might do the trick," I suggested. "You need only take the day off and I will take care of the rest."

He hesitated, possibly not wanting to upset me into spilling his secret, but pulled out a thin folder and pushed it my way. Then the judge entered the room, requiring us to all stand and end our conversation.

"Good morning, good morning," he said, speaking first to the bailiff at his side and then to the prosecutor who had entered the room at the same time, possibly from a private meeting with the judge. He then glanced at our table and frowned at the defence attorney. "Sam, who is this young lady at your table?"

"This … This is …," Sam turned terrified eyes my way.

"Constance Adams, your honour, aiding in the case for the

defence, if it please the court," I said, directing my response at the judge.

"It does not please the court," the judge answered. "Approach the bench, Sam."

Sam bumped into the desk twice trying to get around it and I followed him up to the judge's raised bench, a manoeuvre not lost on the older man.

"Sam, what in blazes is going on? Young lady, I did not ask for you."

"With respect, your honour, if your words are for the defence, then I must be here on behalf of our client," I answered, holding the folder I'd been handed. "My colleague has advised me of his dizziness and sickness and asked me to step in on this case."

"Yes, but who are you?"

"My credentials were sent in a week ago from London and should be on your desk by now," I said to the judge. "Have you not approved them?"

The judge glanced back at his closed office door, perhaps mentally sifting through the paperwork he was guilty of ignoring, and said, "Yes, of course, but Miss Adams, is it? You are not a known party in this case. Who are you?"

"A colleague," sputtered poor Sam, mopping at his brow again. "I must vouch for her, sir, and ask you to give her a day to get caught up on the details of the case, while I … recover."

He said this and then bolted from the room, retching sounds following him as he made it out of the courtroom, but not quite to the bathroom. Either the cocaine or my blackmail had driven the man to vomiting, it didn't really matter which, because his reaction bolstered my claims.

"I wouldn't want to influence a mistrial or delay this case any more than it has been," I said, looking up at the judge. "I wouldn't need more than today to get caught up and represent our client the way he deserves."

The judge glanced over at the prosecutor's table, where the man in the sharp suit stood and said, "We have no objections to the change in representation, your honour, but we would ask for as little delay as possible."

"A half day, Miss Adams," the judge said, hammering his gavel once. "We will see you back in this courtroom at three o'clock in the afternoon and not a moment later."

"I will need to consult with my client and the witnesses," I said, to which the judge nodded at the bailiff.

"Benton, make sure Miss Adams has all the accommodation she requires," he said, coming down from his bench.

I walked over to the prosecutor's desk and he smirked at me, ignoring the hand that I extended. "I thought this case would be over in a week, but without Sam, I think I could be back on the pond by tomorrow morning."

"I appreciate the faith in my abilities," I said acerbically. "In the meantime, your witness list?"

"Just one witness, Miss Adams," he replied, handing me a case file. "The police chief's assistant, Sarah Valentine. Saw the whole thing happen at The Four Ducks pub. Good luck."

CHAPTER 32

THE FIRST THING I did was arrange a private meeting between Annie and her father. I walked into the police station with trepidation, but luckily saw no posters with my face on them, nor newspapers from London lying about, identifying me as the consulting detective from Baker Street. The bailiff was the sympathetic kind, who, out from under the judge's eye, allowed daughter and father a few minutes in the interrogation room alone as we stood outside, before I entered as a representative of the court.

Annie opened the door to the interrogation room, her eyes red from crying, and her father hauled me into a bear hug.

In our long friendship, I'd only met Annie's father a half dozen times because he was always travelling, desperately seeking work to support his three children. He looked exactly like his twin boys, with dirty blonde hair and dark blue eyes, much darker than Annie's own pale blue. The decades of working hard labour meant that despite being in his late fifties, he had the arms and torso of a man half his age, though he also had the scarred hands of someone who dealt with harsh materials and sharp tools.

Now he put a roughened hand on my face so gently that I felt the sting of tears in my own eyes, reminding me of my last moments with my mother. That rare intimacy between a parent and child was something I had sorely missed.

"Portia, I am sorry," he said. "Annie and the boys talk about you all the time. I feel like you're one of my own children and I don't know if I'll ever be able to thank you for letting me say goodbye to my girl here."

"Oh, Daddy," Annie said, dissolving into tears again on a nearby chair.

"And I must ask you to do me another favour," he said, smiling through his tears. "When I am gone, I need you to take care of Annie and my boys. I know you will, I know I almost needn't ask, but since I won't be able to thank you …"

"All right, enough of that talk," I said, pushing him into a chair so that he was beside his weeping daughter. "Mr. Coleson, unless you tell me right now that you killed your foreman, we need to spend every minute we are together finding the actual murderer."

"Of course I didn't kill him!" Coleson said putting his arm around his daughter. "But the assistant … she saw us …"

"Right," I said, pulling out my notebook. "Start from the beginning."

He wove his fingers through Annie's and started his story. "The Four Ducks is where we go after a long day. I've been in that pub three times a week for the entire time I've been out in Sandwell."

"Your foreman, he frequented the pub too?"

"Barris Dubhthaigh, not an easy name to pronounce, and he's a stickler for using his name, something about Gaelic pride," Coleson explained. "He's a diabetic, so he wasn't there as often as us working boys, but he'd show up once a week, buy a round if he was happy with our work."

I twirled my hand to indicate he should keep going with the story.

"So, about a month ago, I was supposed to come home to London for the weekend. You remember, Annie? For the boys' birthday," he said, turning to his daughter for confirmation. She nodded through her tears.

"Barris cancelled our leave, said we were working through the weekend to make up for some missing tools that had slowed our work. The whole crew, no exceptions," Coleson said. "Suffice to say, his buying us a round at The Four Ducks did nothing to improve our mood, mine most of all. Could be that I said some things I shouldn't have. Could be that I threw a mug of ale his way."

Coleson hung his head. "He went to clean up in the men's room and could be I followed him."

Annie rubbed his back in sympathy.

"He was in a stall," Coleson continued. "I swore at him from the sinks. He never came out, never answered. I used the urinal, washed my hands, waited. Nothing. I thought he was hiding in the stall, so I got bored o' course and walked back out of the bathroom, still cussing up a storm. But I swear, I never touched the guy."

"How much time passed between when he went into the bathroom and when you followed him?"

"Couldn't have been more than five minutes."

"And you saw nothing amiss when you walked into the bathroom?"

"I don't know, it's not the cleanest space, if you know what I mean."

"But you know that Barris was in the stall?"

"Well, we all saw him go in and when I followed him, he wasn't at the urinal, so he really had nowhere else he could be. No windows in that room to crawl out of," answered Coleson.

I pulled out the crime scene notes provided by the prosecutor. "According to several witnesses, including Miss Valentine, who was sitting right next to the bathroom 'sober as a priest,' the next person who went in came out yelling that the foreman was dead."

"That was the barman, Eugene," Coleson said. "Owned the bar since his father died. Good man. No grudge against him. He just found Barris lying right inside the bathroom door, sprawled out."

"Why couldn't the barman be the murderer?" Annie asked.

"He opened the door and started yelling, he hadn't even gone into the bathroom," Coleson answered. "We could see Barris lying there, beaten bloody with a lead pipe lying right beside him."

Annie winced and her father apologized to her. "Before I could do more than stumble over to the body, that Valentine girl is screeching that I be held down before I hurt anyone else. But I tell you both, I couldn't have done it, even if I were angrier than I've ever been."

"Of course not, Dad," she whispered, her eyes on me. "Portia, what do we do?"

"We start by talking to this Valentine woman and find out why she was there," I said, circling her name on my notepad.

Coleson looked between us with confusion. "Valentine? Why?"

"I'm betting that she did not frequent the pub," I said, loading the notebook back in my satchel as I spoke. "Seeing as she was, as notes describe it, sober as a priest?"

"Who goes to a bar and doesn't drink?" Annie asked, getting her coat on.

"You can stay with your father, Annie, I can …"

"No way. If this witch is lying, I want to be there," Annie said, giving her father a kiss on the brow. "Plus, if you're right, which you always are, he'll be coming home to London with me tonight."

According to Benton the bailiff, Sarah Valentine was scheduled to be called as a witness in the afternoon, so he knew exactly where she was. He knocked on the front door to her upstairs flat, introduced us, and promised to wait outside the door to keep everyone else out while we conducted our interview.

Valentine led us into her small sitting room, rubbing at her arms as if she were cold. The room was immaculate but for a large cabinet at the back of the room that had dishes and teacups stacked on top of it rather than inside, making it stand out for its clutter.

"I've just put the tea kettle back on, so it should be just a moment," she said, her quiet voice matching her demeanour. Her clothing was very modest for a woman about the same age as Annie and me, bordering on puritanical with a high-necked blouse that got a lot of use, and a severe bun in her dark hair.

"Miss Valentine, I'm sorry to be asking you this so late in this case's progression. I am sure you are tired of answering the same questions over and over again," I said.

She nodded, but took a deep breath in, as if steeling herself for the worst. Looking at Annie and the way she was glaring at the woman, I could hardly blame her.

"What were you doing at The Four Ducks pub?"

"As I told the police and the prosecutor," the woman replied, barely lifting her eyes from her lap, but speaking in a louder voice, "I was to meet my father there."

"But you don't drink," I pointed out.

"No, I do not," she affirmed. "But my father does and some-times asks that I help walk him back home. I felt it was safer to wait inside for my father than outside."

"Then your father was also a witness to the murder?" Annie asked.

"He was not in a state of mind to testify," Sarah said, glancing up and then right back down at her hands in her lap. "Not many of them were, other than the barman and myself. Hence how I find myself in the situation I am in."

"And can you tell me what exactly you saw that night?"

"When I came in Mr. Coleson was — I'm sorry to say, Miss Coleson — deep in his cups," she said, looking guilty for saying so. "I've witnessed that level of drunkenness many times before. It almost always leads to violence and it must be addressed, lest he take it out on someone else."

I interjected here before Annie could rise to her father's defence. "I did not ask what you assumed, Miss Valentine, I asked exactly what you saw. If we can stick to the facts, I think this will go easier."

She flushed and nodded. "Of course, I do not mean to make this harder on Miss Coleson at all. The facts. I came into the pub, did not see my father, and so sat at a table away from the bar."

"And why did you choose that table?"

"The only other chairs were in front of the bar itself and they were all taken. Also, this table had a single seat and I didn't want to be engaged by a drunken patron."

"Drawing on your experience?" I suggested with a smile.

She gave me a small smile back, appreciating my support of the shared strategy amongst women. "Yes. And when I sat down I saw Mr. Coleson pointing at the foreman, Mr. Dubhthaigh, and cussing at him. I wasn't entirely clear on the issue, but it seemed that several of the men had unkind things to say about the foreman."

"Your pronunciation of that name is better than ours, Miss Valentine," Annie remarked before I could. "Is it in your family?"

Valentine nodded, still not meeting Annie's eyes, and answered in a quieter voice, barely discernible to my ears. "Yes, on my mother's side. She made sure we were fluent in Gaelic, even when the schools were against it."

"Go on please, Miss Valentine," I said.

"Mr. Coleson threw a drink at Mr. Dubhthaigh, forcing the poor man to get cleaned up. He was quite soaked and the barman and another man restrained Mr. Coleson."

"Restrained for how long?"

"Not long. Certainly not long enough for Mr. Dubhthaigh to finish cleaning himself up."

"Did anyone else leave the bar or enter the men's room?"

"No, like I said, the men sitting at the bar held Mr. Coleson, tried to calm him, and then everyone sat back down as they were before."

The sound of the kettle whistling brought a smile to my lips, mostly because I heard it, distinctly. Valentine got up with a jump, but not before I heard the whistle stop on its own. She had the tea back in front of us before I asked my next question.

"And this is when your father came in?"

The teacup she was handing to Annie shook in her hand, the answer I had been waiting for.

"Yes, my father came into the pub while all of this was happening," Valentine said, completing the transaction of handing the teacup to Annie and sitting back in her chair. "And then Mr. Coleson went into the men's room."

"And what did you do while Mr. Coleson and Mr. Dubhthaigh were in there together?" I asked.

"What do you mean?"

"Did you speak to your father? Did you leave your seat? What did you do?" I pressed.

"I … I did nothing," she said, her nervousness back. "I heard Mr. Coleson continue to shout at Mr. Dubhthaigh. And then I saw him come back out, waving his hands."

"Waving his hands?"

"Yes, shaking them off. I think he had washed them."

I took note of that. "And where was your father?"

"He was in the pub, as I said," Valentine answered immediately.

"Yes, but Portia is asking where," Annie said, sitting forward a bit in her chair. "Was he also at the bar, ordering a drink? Or was he sitting with you?"

"He was … Yes, he ordered a drink at the bar," Valentine said, nodding.

I flipped through my notes. "I don't see that in the barman's statement or in the receipts for the night …"

"Or maybe he just sat at the bar and didn't order," Valentine said, swallowing nervously. "I couldn't be sure of that. I was, after all, beside the men's room where it was quite loud."

"Right and then after Mr. Coleson came out of the men's room, did you see anything?" I asked.

"See anything? Other than Mr. Coleson shaking his hands of water? No."

"Wait, so you think my father killed someone in the men's room, washed his hands, and sat down for another drink?" Annie asked, incredulous.

"He was deep in his cups, as I said," Valentine answered defensively. "The next thing I saw was the barman coming out from behind the bar, opening the door to the men's room, and immediately calling for help."

I read out from the notes. "Yes, the barman says you became quite hysterical at the sight of Dubhthaigh's body and begged the rest of the patrons to restrain Mr. Coleson, lest he hurt anyone else."

Annie took a sip of tea before saying, "The barman would not have had time or opportunity to beat Mr. Dubhthaigh."

"Not at all," Valentine agreed, mimicking Annie and taking a small sip of her own tea. "He opened the door and didn't even step over the threshold. Mr. Dubhthaigh was there for all of us to see."

"But when my father exited the men's room, Mr. Dubhthaigh wasn't there lying at the door," Annie pointed out. "You surely would have seen him step over a body as he left."

"I … I suppose he was not. But perhaps he dragged himself to the door. That's what the prosecutor said. That Mr. Dubhthaigh had been left for dead and dragged himself to the door after Mr. Coleson left."

"And when the barman raised the alarm, everyone came running?" Annie asked, looking through the notes in front of me, pulling up the witness statements.

Sarah Valentine nodded. "I didn't move. I couldn't. It was too horrible. But yes, I saw everyone run to the men's room door, including Mr. Coleson."

"And your father?" I asked.

Valentine nodded quickly and then threw in a "Yes, of course, my father was there as well. Surely that is in your witness notes? The police talked to him at length."

"Yes, I see his statement, but I'm asking where he came from — the barstool where he was sitting?"

Annie put down her cup when Valentine nodded, glancing over her shoulder. "Could I get some more sugar from the pantry, Miss Valentine?"

"I … Let me get it," she said, standing hastily.

I nodded at Annie as she waited for Sarah to leave the room and then followed her. I was unsurprised when she came back in the company of a large man.

"Mr. Valentine I presume," I said, extending my hand.

The man grimaced at me. "I don't shake hands with the likes of you."

"Women, lawyers, or people who disrupt your plans?" I asked as Annie moved around behind me.

He took a step forward and I held my ground. "I will remind you, sir, that the bailiff stands outside your daughter's door and would surely hear us when we scream, which I intend to, loudly, should you take another step in our direction. And you wouldn't want an officer of the courts in here, would you, snooping around?"

He looked at the door, the cabinet at the back of the room, and then back at me with a menacing look. "I think you're done here."

"We are," I agreed. "I believe I have all the information I need, and Miss Valentine, I suggest you return with us now to the courthouse."

Mr. Valentine grasped his daughter's upper arm, causing her to wince. "She isn't goin' anywhere."

"That's what you think," Annie said, opening the front door. "Bailiff, we need to take Sarah Valentine with us back to the courthouse. Could you please advise Mr. Valentine of the judge's orders?"

Valentine dropped his daughter's arm as soon as the door opened and she looked a little faint, so I stepped up to her, wrapping an arm around her shoulder, leading her to the door where the bailiff and Annie stood.

I closed the door on the furious man in the apartment, handed the shaking daughter over to Annie's capable arms, and said to the bailiff, "We need a police force here right now. I believe if you were to position men outside this door, you would catch Mr. Valentine attempting to leave this apartment with explosives that he stole from Mr. Dubhthaigh. And Benton, I'd get them here immediately unless you want to stop him by yourself."

Astonished as he looked, he did as I bade, running to the nearest police box on the block.

"Portia …," Annie said, her eyes wide. "What in the world …"

"Dubhthaigh is the true Gaelic form of O'Duffy, Annie," I said, leading the women a safe distance from the door which could burst open at any moment. "Your father stumbled into a local in-fight of the Irish Resistance."

"Miss Valentine, you have been harshly used by your father, both physically and now morally," I said to the pale woman at Annie's side. "You must right this. It will be as simple as admitting that your father told you to sit at that table and that he was not in the pub until after Mr. Dubhthaigh was discovered bleeding on the floor of the men's room."

She gaped at me. "How … How did you …?"

"Your father must have heard about the bombs through your mother's family. Maybe he knows more Gaelic than they think he does. And not sharing in the Irish's rather violent petitions for equality, decided he could sell the bombs for a pretty price," I said, nodding at the bailiff who repositioned himself outside the Valentines' door with his billy club out and in his hands. "He arranged you as the perfect credible witness and hid in the men's room waiting for Dubhthaigh, knowing the man had diabetes and frequented the toilets more than the rest of us. As soon as the poor man opened the stall he was knocked out with the lead pipe and positioned on the toilet so that his feet were showing beneath the stall. Mr. Coleson came in, berated Dubhthaigh some more from outside the stall at the urinals and, not being engaged on the other side, left. At which point Valentine finished his bloody work and kicked poor Dubhthaigh to the floor and left him there for the next man to discover."

"But where did Mr. Valentine go?" Annie broke in.

"He stayed in the stall, probably crouched over the toilet until Dubhthaigh was dragged into the main bar," I said, watching Sarah's face crumble. "I'll bet that you were so distracted by the fracas, Miss Valentine, that you were surprised to see your father suddenly appear as one of the men around Dubhthaigh's body. Did you wonder when he had come in?"

"I wasn't sure, I swear," she said, her croaking voice coming through a bit to my ears. "I was so nervous, sitting there, and then … the shouting … and so much blood … and then my father, he told me what I had to say. He said he'd kill me if I didn't."

"And the bombs?" Annie asked.

"The same ones the police are searching for in London, Annie, though I don't know how many of them made it up here. I'm not sure of some of the details still, but if those are the same mines discovered at the bomb sites in London, Valentine's motive will be enough to get your father released," I replied, pulling my hat lower over my eyes at the arrival of the police. "Can you manage this with the local police? I'd rather not take the chance. And have them check the cabinet for the missing tools from the mine. Valentine might have had the foresight to instigate the anger against the foreman."

Annie nodded confidently, leaving Sarah with me and stepping forward to speak to the bailiff and the two officers.

"You and I must regroup with that useless defence attorney, I think. Now that the police are involved, I must step back, but we will solve two parental issues today: we will free Annie's father, and start the process to get yours where he belongs. Behind bars."

CHAPTER 33

SAM WAS ACTUALLY A moderately useful lawyer once you got a whole pot of coffee in him and walked him through the evidence twice. With the revised statement from Sarah Valentine and the new testimony from the police chief, fresh from retrieving nine Russian-made bombs from a duffle bag in the Valentine flat plus the stolen tools, it took under an hour to secure Mr. Coleson's release in the judge's chambers. I was basically ignored, the focus on Sam and the prosecutor, who were thrilled with this new level of drama in their sleepy town and happy to let the Colesons and their odd lady friend drift away.

We left the courthouse with the assurance that Mr. Valentine would be charged with several crimes, including the premeditated murder of Barris Dubhthaigh, younger brother to Éamon O'Duffy.

Only Benton the bailiff stopped me on our way out. "Constance Adams from London. I will not forget that name."

I shook his hand, and suggested he forget it right away, hoping his admiration wouldn't turn to bile when he found out that I was being sought by Box 850.

We made the last train to London with minutes to spare, Annie and her father sharing one bench and I on the other side in the train car, unable to restrain my grin at their relief and joy.

"How will we ever thank you?" Mr. Coleson said finally, reaching for my hand.

"If you truly think of me as family, Mr. Coleson, no thanks are necessary," I said, squeezing his hand. "In fact, by helping you, I've probably condemned you to weeks of surveillance from Box 850."

He waved that off. "They can watch us all they want, but they'd better not get too close, or they'll get an earful for the way they're treating you."

Annie shook her head at her father. "We just got you out of jail for running your mouth off. Can you please keep your opinions to yourself?"

"How can we stay silent while our Portia is being chased out of her home and business?" he demanded of her. "No, you have to give me something to do, Portia. Something that will help you. Or I may run mad."

I smiled at him and Annie. "I have the perfect thing. Can you and the boys stay at my Baker Street apartment for a bit? You will be surveilled wherever you are, to be honest, until I clear my name and therefore your association with me. I need someone to dissuade Box 850 from picking through my life, and I need people to help watch Brian."

I quickly filled them in on the situation with my partner, the addiction to opioids, and Gavin's involvement in our troubles. They had matching reactions, from sympathy to horror to anger, looking at each other before promising to take care of Brian and his family on my behalf.

I wrote a note for my grandmother explaining all of this, and also begging her for a stipend for the Colesons while they did this work for me. It wouldn't be easy to persuade Mr. Coleson to take the money, but if anyone could do it, my grandmother could. Mr. Coleson agreed to take the note to my grandmother before scooping up the boys and taking over my flat. He threw his arms around Annie and me, squeezing us tight and giving us both a kiss on the forehead before we left him, getting off at Kensal Green, well before the main London stops.

"Are you sure about this, Annie?" I asked her again, following her lead as she hailed a cab.

"No, but like you said, our choices are limited," she replied, ushering me into the car, and giving the directions to the cabbie.

We pulled up at a nondescript row of townhouses and I followed Annie up the stairs to observe three mailboxes marked only with A, B, and C. No names or other identification. I guessed that if I were to walk up to the other townhouses, this might be a common occurrence.

"You promised not to be critical," Annie said, holding the key in her hand, and I nodded, for what choice did I have?

The townhouse was dark and Annie didn't turn on a light until she got to the second floor where she stepped with more confidence, unlocking a door directly off the main stairs and flicking a switch on. Inside was a large single room with expensive furnishings, a small kitchen, a tiny water closet, a small sofa, and a king-sized bed. I bit my tongue from saying anything, so tired that I really wished my brain wasn't cataloguing the space for what it obviously was.

"He's good to me, Portia," Annie said, crossing her arms over her chest, her bare feet buried in the shag rug under the sofa, comforting herself with its familiar softness. "And his wife is barely holding on to her sanity. She's more of a child than a wife."

"I'd heard the rumours," I agreed, taking off my coat and satchel and making my way to the kitchen to pour a glass of water for each of us.

I handed her the glass and she stared at me pensively before drinking from it. "Then you have nothing to say?"

"I have nothing to say," I agreed. "Save to thank you for finding us somewhere safe to spend the night. I haven't had that in a very long time."

Her shoulders came down at that. Not all the way, but enough that I redoubled my efforts to ignore the clues all around me that spoke of Annie not being the only woman this rich peer had brought here. She was just the latest conquest and when her charms were overshadowed by a newer, younger version, she would be put aside, just like the others. I said none of this aloud, said nothing of the remnants left behind by a young nurse, and the book forgotten by a woman of Indian descent, possibly a tutor by profession.

Annie in the meantime had gone to the closet to pull out a robe. "Why don't you have a wash up? I can warm up some soup or something if you like."

By the time I was back out, two bowls of soup and a small crust of bread were laid out on the coffee table in front of the sofa. Annie had several papers spread out in front of her and was reading all of them at once it seemed.

"You were right about Gavin, he's right on the front lines," she said, seeing me.

She pushed a copy of the *Intelligencer* my way, where I could see a photo of a group of men exiting Downing Street. The men walking in front were the focus of the shot, but bringing up the rear, deep in conversation, were Gavin and Ramsay MacDonald — the prime minister easily recognizable for his shock of thick white hair and uneven moustache. Gavin looked the part of a diplomat, his suit tailored in crisp lines, hugging his shoulders. Several newspapers had captured this moment from different angles, some showing Gavin, some not.

"How is he even back in London? Doesn't the Yard have open cases he has to answer for?" she asked between bites of soup.

"Gavin knows that, it's why he's back under the protection of diplomatic immunity," I answered. "But I wonder what he's working on. Officially, he seems to be working with the coalition government as some kind of intermediary between the German and British governments."

"But unofficially?"

"I'm worried he might be the one supplying the British government with arms," I said.

Annie whistled under her breath. "Well, that's a promotion if I've ever heard of one."

We finished our soup deep in our own thoughts and I promised to join Annie in bed as soon as I finished reading the papers. I found two stories describing the scene Lancaster and I had run away from, the journalists describing the unsolved murders of Harold Digby, an unidentified teenaged girl (Ilsa), and Constable Rory McKinnon. Neither the spy nor I made the papers at all.

The bomber hadn't struck again while I was out of London, which was as I'd predicted. I only hoped that the threats wouldn't resume now that I was back. If the bomber was actually aware of Box 850's suspicions, then they would be happy to tie me to the bombing by only committing or threatening the crimes while I was in town to take the blame. Of course, that would give me more data because the fact that Box 850 was pursuing me at all was not a widely known fact. The posters around town didn't describe why I was a person of interest, only that I was. But if the bomber was in fact linked to the Secret Intelligence Service or Scotland Yard, then why were some of the bombs showing up in the Black Country? I pressed on the bridge of my nose, feeling a headache coming on and looking at the bed where Annie slept. I closed the newspaper wearily and crawled in beside her, leaving these open questions to the kindness of the morning light.

CHAPTER 34

"I LOOK RIDICULOUS," ANNIE said, staring at herself in the mirror.

"You look plain," I corrected with a smile. "Something you have never experienced before, I admit, but not ridiculous."

"This wig makes me look sixteen," she complained, poking at the mass of curly brown hair under the newsboy hat.

"No, that's the lack of makeup and the fact that you're wearing mismatched clothes," I said. "But this will get you into the War Office without a second glance. Students are always coming in and out of there on various research projects."

"Meanwhile, you look like …"

"You," I said, fluffing my pretty blonde wig, a replica of Annie's natural short bob. I had borrowed her clothes from the day before, though I had kept my flat boots because of our height difference. I wouldn't be able to fool someone who knew Annie well, but an acquaintance to be sure.

She glared at me in the mirror. "Only for you, Portia Adams."

"You will remember my instructions concerning The Wool and Weaver?" I prompted her, helping her don my father's old coat.

"I will pretend to shop at the fabric store until I am sure I am not being followed," she replied with a nod. "And if I pop upstairs, I can change out of these ridiculous clothes before we meet."

I followed her out the front door of the flat where she stopped me. "Here, you keep the key in case anything goes wrong. I can always go home to Spital Street after all. And Portia, do be careful."

I promised and she was on her way down the stairs and out the front door of the townhouse paid for by her rich boyfriend. I waited five minutes and then followed her, exiting the front door with my umbrella open and heading straight to the train station. I got off a stop before my destination and walked the rest of the way, making sure to smile at the newspaper boys as I bought today's paper. I wanted them to remember a friendly blonde rather than the introspective brunette hiding underneath. I took the back stairs into the building and opened the paper to the crossword puzzle, writing in answers as I walked until I was at the door to the office I knew well. I knocked and entered at the same time, surprising the occupants in a rather provocative position.

"Oh dear," I muttered, closing the door and turning to face the people as they leapt apart.

"What in blazes do you think you're ...," Inspector Michaels started to say, and then did a double take, actually seeing who it was.

"Portia!" my cousin Heather mouthed and then she ran to me, her blouse still half-unbuttoned, her state of dress forgotten for the moment.

Michaels was stunned, but his hands were still moving, doing up the buttons on his shirt and straightening his hair out. "Adams, what the Hell are you doing here?"

I struggled out of Heather's bear hug, only managing to negotiate half my body away to answer, "I'm here to help and to get some help, Inspector."

"You can speak again, Portia," Heather said, holding my face in her hands, her smile as wide as her face. "Amélie? I knew she could help you."

"In more ways than one, Doc."

I heard the knock at the door behind me, but not the words of whoever knocked, and Michaels fairly leapt past the two of us to stick his head out and answer.

"You're not safe here," Heather said, leading me to the opposite corner of the office and closing the blinds before speaking again.

"Doc, I can speak again, yes, but my hearing's still not one hundred percent. No whispering," I said, forcing her to turn back towards me.

"Your grandmother told us she had sent you to Italy for your own safety," she repeated, braiding her long silvery hair into a single plait.

I had no doubt that Irene Adler was planting clues of my escape all over Europe so as to confuse the Secret Intelligence Service. No matter how angry my grandmother was with me, she always had my back.

"As you can see, I am not. Meanwhile, Gavin is back in town and he's up to something," I said in reply.

"Gavin, your … ex-boyfriend?"

"Wait, start over," Michaels said, rejoining the conversation. "Why aren't you in Italy?"

As quickly as I could I brought my allies up to speed. When I got to the part about Brian, Michaels interrupted me.

"He didn't mention that Whitaker was behind his dereliction of duty. I wouldn't have been so hard on him if he'd said something about that," Michaels said, reaching for a cigar.

I wasn't surprised that Brian had taken the full blame upon

himself, but I wasn't going to let Gavin get away with his manipulations.

"I docked Dawes' pay, but his shrink spoke up for him, said he was on the mend, so he's still on payroll," Michaels said. "Threw up twice in my wastepaper basket, by the way."

"His shrink?"

"An older Dutch man with quite an accent and an immaculate beard," Heather explained, describing one of Holmes' favourite disguises. "He came with Brian to the Yard, explained the course of treatment he was administering. Your boyfriend is lucky to have him. Said Dr. Watson set them up."

I smiled at that reference because of course Sherlock Holmes had been referred many times by the late Dr. Watson, just not the young Dr. Watson Heather was talking about.

"Constable Dawes is meeting with the officer in charge of Éamon O'Duffy," Michaels put in. "You didn't have anything to add to that angle did you?"

With a sigh I filled them in on my trip to Sandwell to exonerate Mr. Coleson of his involvement with the Barris Dubhthaigh murder that in turn led to the discovery of the bombs being used to torment Londoners.

"At some point, you and this Lancaster fellow will have to come in and give your statements. I don't care who you are or who you're running from."

"Of course," I agreed. "But in the meantime, I think we can all agree that Whitaker ..."

"Whitaker is protected by all kinds of international law," Michaels pointed out, puffing around his cigar, something that made it harder to read his lips. "Can't even bring him in for questioning while he's got that blasted diplomatic immunity. All we can do is expel him from the Kingdom, but there's no way the government is going to back us on that. If he's helping them get weapons — which, by the way, is ridiculous. He's a kid. No way he's built a network of black market weapons pirated in the few years he's been out of our sight."

"I'm not the only one who thinks so," I said, glancing at Heather.

Michaels snorted, "If you mean your little journalist friend ..."

"No, someone you hate but can't help but believe," I interrupted.

Michaels finally understood that I was talking about Holmes, someone Heather still didn't know was a part of my family, but was probably suspecting at this point. I did not want to imagine my cousin psychoanalyzing the motivations of the Holmes side of my family. Not now, maybe not ever.

"Do you at least have someone following him?"

"Of course we do!" Michaels blustered. "I may not be able to bring him in, but I trust him about as far as I can throw him. He's got round-the-clock surveillance between Downing Street and The Gore Hotel where they're all staying."

"What aren't you two telling me?" Heather asked, looking back and forth between us. "Why are you having Gavin followed when you don't think that he's a danger?"

"He's a danger," Michaels and I said, almost in unison.

"And in the meantime, what about this ruddy bomber?" Michaels said, tapping flakes onto his desk which Heather quickly swept into his rubbish basket. "It sounds like a few of the bombs are in hand in Sandwell, which is fantastic, but that still leaves ... a half-dozen unaccounted for?"

"Seven by my count, but that's based on the questionable memory of a pilfering colonel, as relayed to me by a spy," I said, watching as Michaels riffled through his desk for a file.

"Thirty bombs of this type in total," he said, reading from a coffee-stained sheet of paper. "According to Colonel Collins, substantiated by his daughter, Alisha ..."

"Wait, who?"

"Alisha Collins, daughter to Colonel Collins," Michaels answered with a frown.

"Who is related to Major Collins?" I said, stepping forward to look at the sheet of paper.

"Not sure, who is Major Collins?" Michaels asked.

"Husband to Heddy Collins and somehow connected to Lancaster," I replied.

"Could be. Military service is common in families as you know," Heather pointed out, leaning over the paper as well now. "Why is Major Collins significant? Could he be the bomber?"

"No, according to Lancaster, he was killed sometime after the war," I replied, trying to fit the pieces together and coming up with a very strange solution. "I need to speak to Heddy Collins and I need to do it with Annie and Lancaster."

"Fine, we can arrange that through Downing Street. You said she works there," Michaels said, raising a hand when Heather protested. "We can't stop her, pet, you know Portia Adams is like one of those bloody Mounties. She always gets her man."

"Actually, that's a common misconception. The RCMP slogan is 'Uphold the Right,' but I'm happy to accept the comparison and agree to that arrangement, especially if you could set it up somewhere private where the Secret Intelligence Service can't find me ..."

"Ah, not exactly."

I looked at Heather, because surely I was hearing things, but she just shrugged.

"I'll get the widow Collins, but you have to talk to Colonel Kell. Convince him of your innocence," Michaels said, removing the cigar from his mouth so I had no doubt as to what he was saying. "I can't lie to the Secret Intelligence Service and do my job. You agree to meet with Heddy Collins and Kell together or I have to arrest you here and now."

I closed my eyes against my dread and agreed.

CHAPTER 35

"WHAT DO YOU MEAN you're going to meet with Kell?" Lancaster repeated, his arms folded over his chest. He had shaved and was wearing a leather jacket over a white button-up with dark blue jeans. Suffice to say, I was both happy and unhappy that we were the first to arrive at the fabric store.

"I had to give Michaels my word that I would go directly from this meeting to Kell," I said, standing on the other side of the window and watching for the rest of our party where two days earlier I had waited with Brian hidden behind boxes while he retched and suffered.

"You can't do it," Lancaster said. "The man has ways of making people disappear."

"He can't make me disappear; we'll be with Scotland Yard's finest," I said. "Now, you promised to tell me about Heddy Collins as soon as I could describe her connection. I think you knew it all along. Her father-in-law is the same Colonel Collins who misplaced the bombs, isn't it?"

"You mean to take your constable with you?"

I nodded. "Answer the question, Lancaster. I need to know."

"Does he know about us?"

My heart thudding so hard I believed I might hear it, I said, "There is no us. There is a shared goal of clearing our names …"

"There is a deep attraction that we've given in to on one or two occasions," he interrupted, sliding a hand around my waist.

"Mistakenly," I corrected, pressing away from him.

"I prefer to call it irresistibly," he said, leaning down to kiss my neck.

"Did you kill Major Collins?"

That was a guaranteed way to kill a mood and it did the trick. Lancaster stiffened, raising disbelieving eyes to mine. "What did you say?"

"It's my hearing that's damaged, Lancaster, not yours," I pointed out. "Enough dancing around this. You and Major Collins were on assignment at some point and he was killed. You were blamed. Were they wrong to blame you?"

Lancaster dropped his hands from my waist, applying them to his hair instead, rubbing at it before answering. "They weren't wrong. It was my fault."

"Explain."

He sat down on a box, his head in his hands. When he finally looked up he said, "You were right. I had an affair with my best mate's wife. Heddy Collins and I were lovers. Is that what you wanted to hear?"

"Not specifically, no," I admitted. "But it's a start. You were lovers. Did you kill Major Collins in self-defence when he attacked you for cuckolding him?"

"You don't understand, he never knew. He trusted us both implicitly," Lancaster said. "Look, Collins was a good man. He fell for Heddy while we were on assignment in Lisburn. She was a social pariah in that little North Ireland town — she's German and it was after the war. But her parents were killed by the Prussian secret police, so she's no friend to the Nazis or Hitler. Poor girl changed her name twice, but the accent lingered. It's actually how they became close — Collins would help her practise her English and Gaelic."

I nodded. The war had divided Europe in many ways, but everyone blamed the Germans equally, regardless of their personal beliefs.

"I'm surprised you had time to engage in an affair," I said.

"The Lisburn assignment came up dry," Lancaster admitted. "The families were so powerfully established that after several months we were making no progress.

"She was there the night he was killed," he continued, closing his eyes as if the scene was replaying behind his eyelids. "She was a waitress at a seedy pub. Collins was the talker, the front man. I was his back-up. It was much harder to blend in as a Black man in that small a town, but I was travelling as a singer in a band. That way the tour would bring me round the area and I could check in with Collins on the sly. Heddy helped us with that."

"She knew you were spies?"

Lancaster shrugged, opening his eyes. "She was a bright woman. Put it together on her own. Truth is she was bound to find out with all the time she and Collins were spending together."

"And you spending time with her as well."

"Yes, though she instigated that, I swear," he said. "And I wasn't the one who confirmed her suspicions. That was Collins."

"Go back to the night Collins was killed."

Lancaster winced, but continued his tale. "He was sitting at the bar, flirting with Heddy as usual, and I was watching from a booth near the back. One of our informants comes in and Collins gives me the signal to cover their chat."

Lancaster stood up and grabbed his hat off the box next to us, adjusted the brim and then put it back down to demonstrate this signal. "So, I call Heddy over to take my order, acting more drunk than I am, causing her to get the bartender and a few of the barflies involved in escorting me out of the pub."

"This has worked in the past?"

"No one wants the likes of me in the pub in the first place, so it's not hard to convince them to make me leave," he answered dryly.

"The barman and his helpers give me some advice as to where I should take my sorry self and go back inside the way they came. The thing was, it was up to me how I gave Collins space to have his talk. And I chose this one. Heddy was helping me off the street, when we heard the shots," Lancaster said.

"Collins."

"Collins and our informant," Lancaster answered. "Shot up like … I can't describe it." He shuddered. "No one saw anything because most of the bar was outside with me and Heddy. The hit man had been hiding in the shadows like me, waiting for the opportunity. I had missed him. That was my job. To back up Collins. I failed because I was watching Collins and Heddy at the bar like a jealous lover — which I was."

"You know who it was?"

"Absolutely, they arrested her two days later. She'd discovered our little operation and took matters into her own hands for the good of the community. Never saw a day in jail. We had to hightail it out of there."

"You and Heddy?"

"Me and Heddy."

"And then what?"

"Heddy was distraught," Lancaster explained. "She'd lost her hard-won employment — something that wasn't easy to recover from, being a German woman — and she'd lost the man she loved. I had, or thought I had, the service to go back to, but she had nothing."

"So, you procured her a marriage certificate."

Lancaster looked slightly surprised, but a smile started to drift across his face. "Best thing I ever did. I could at least give her the safety of a good English family and a pension, and I believe Collins would have married her if he had lived."

"And you brought her back to London and introduced her to the Collins family."

"I did and Kell helped me get her a job at the mayor's office," Lancaster said, sitting back down. "She parlayed that into the job at Downing Street herself. Told you she was bright."

"And Box 850?"

"Blamed me for losing Collins that way and ruining a three-month operation," Lancaster answered, pulling out a cigarette and lighting it.

"Heddy testified against you," I guessed.

Lancaster nodded, taking a long drag. "I don't blame her. She loved Collins and I left him alone. And she had to come out on the right side of this or risk being extradited or something worse. So, Box 850 disavowed me. Said I stood out too much to be a useful spy anyway. Turns out Collins had been putting in good words for me for years. Without him, I had lost … everything. And I guess Kell was right about me, because a month after I was thrown out, the Service started to make real progress in Northern Ireland."

"But with the bombs going missing from the Collins residence, surely you suspected Heddy?" I said.

"I know our relationship will colour your impression of my objectivity, but I'm telling you, Heddy Collins is no terrorist.

She has no reason to draw attention to herself that way — imagine!" he said, standing again to look out the window. "She is a master at laying low. She's been doing it her whole life. If bombs started going off all over London that could connect back to her in-laws, it would be her absolute nightmare."

"Her absolute nightmare," I repeated, standing up to pace in front of the window.

"You believe me?" Lancaster asked, pulling me close again.

"I believe you have been taken in by a smart woman and that we've been misled by another," I answered. "But I believe you to be honest, if that's what you're asking."

"Taken in by … Portia haven't you been listening?"

"Amélie," I said, pushing harder against Lancaster and pointing at the woman's figure stealing between the buildings. "Why isn't she coming here? Didn't you tell her to make sure she wasn't being …"

"Followed," muttered Lancaster pointing at the two shadowy bodies that were right behind her. She noticed them too and started to run, darting into The Wool and Weaver.

Lancaster took off ahead of me and he was down the stairs and around the fabric store by the time I caught sight of him again, lying prostrate halfway across the street. A quick check revealed that his pulse was strong and he was breathing on his own, he must have just been knocked out. Which meant we weren't alone. I pretended to be oblivious to any other presence and began to pull Lancaster behind some trash bins. Then I smelled alcohol and felt a hand I expected grip my shoulder. I grabbed the arm and pulled, flipping the man over my crouched body. What I couldn't fight was the two other men and the hand that pressed a sickly smelling cloth over my nose and mouth. I curled forward and then smacked my head back fast, hitting my second assailant in the jaw. He released me and I dropped to my knees, my head swimming. I crawled back to Lancaster and collapsed on his chest.

CHAPTER 36

"YOU NEARLY BROKE THAT thug's jaw," said a voice out of the darkness.

I groaned and tried to sit up.

"Gently now, Portia, that form of chloroform packs a punch almost as strong as you."

"Gavin?"

"That's right. How's your head?"

"I can hear you," I said, allowing him to help me into a sitting position. "I must be dreaming about you again."

"Dreaming about me again? I'm flattered."

"That's what you said last time," I answered, my eyes growing used to the dark. We were in a train car again, but it wasn't moving. Thank God.

"Last time?" he asked, crouching at my legs that I could now feel were bound in handcuffs, along with my wrists. "Pray, what were we doing the last time you dreamed of me?"

Gavin wasn't the lecherous type. I knew I had been his very first lover, but his smile was a little suggestive. Something was wrong with this dream. This train car smelled like fish. And he smelled wrong too. Like spice and flowers.

"When did you start wearing cologne?" I asked, noticing

that the doors were on the short side, not sliding along the long side, and revising my jail to a shipping container, not a train car.

"Ah, my fiancée insists on it," he said ruefully, gently moving my bangs so they didn't hang in my face. "She's been experimenting with various smells. Speaking of experimenting, I like this new hair."

"*Mouchoir de Monsieur*," I whispered. This wasn't a dream. It was a nightmare.

"Why yes," he answered. "Made by the same master perfumers as the scent you're wearing I believe."

"But that isn't why you wear it," I said, staring at him, trying to see the man I had loved. "You wear it for her."

"I do," he admitted. "And I'm doing this for her as well."

"You're doing this for yourself," I corrected, grasping his chin with my bound hands. "At least admit that to me if not to anyone else. I am a thorn in your side. It's why you took my speech from me."

"Temporarily, my dear, and only when your chosen career had already put you in danger. I took advantage of the situation, I did not cause it," he said, not fighting my hands. "I needed your mind otherwise engaged. I always intended to wean you off the pills and I knew that your hearing would return, and look, it has. Patience was all that was required. But now? Well, you've forced my hand. I really can't have you solving this bomb case. Not now. I am too close to my next conquest."

"Selling arms to the British government?" I asked with a shake of my head. "What are you doing, Gavin?"

"There's a war coming, or hadn't you picked up on the signs? I'm helping our side, Portia, or whichever side pays the most, to be frank. Right now, that's the Brits."

"But you're representing the Austrians while dealing under the table with the Brits?"

Gavin shrugged. "Sides change all the time. And the people who are supplying me with weapons aren't very dear to the Brits, so the Austrian diplomat thing allows for me to launder the arms through my position with very little fuss. Honestly, it works out well for king and country. Surely you can't complain."

"What did you do with Lancaster?" I asked.

"Lancaster?" he answered, edging a little closer. "What about the redoubtable constable?"

"Brian is safe from your manipulations," I said with more confidence than I actually felt. Surely between him and my grand-father, they would have avoided Gavin and his lackeys. "Lancaster was lying on the street last I saw him, another victim of your special brand of chemistry."

"I'll tell you what, I'll let you choose," Gavin said. "Which one of your suitors would you like to spend your last moments with?"

"I choose you," I said, putting my bound arms around his neck and kissing him soundly on the mouth. He didn't fight me, leaning into my embrace, tasting exactly as I remembered, that combination of peppermint and scotch. I pulled him further into the cushioned chair I was bound in and he pulled away first, looking at me with astonishment.

"Portia, you know why we can't be together," he said, inches from my mouth.

"I do," I admitted. "But I wouldn't condemn anyone else to die with me here."

"I meant your last moments of freedom — I could never kill you," he said. "But I can leave you here to be retrieved by Kell's local agents. I'll even leave your favourite satchel there by the door with one of those Russian bombs you've been searching for. Now, don't give me that look. I guarantee that even though it looks bad, it will, in fact, exonerate you. Eventually."

He leaned in and then thought better of it and kissed me on the forehead. "Give Annie my regards. I'm very glad you managed to save her father from the noose. Now you'll have to do your best to save her from the peer she's playing house with."

CHAPTER 37

I SQUINTED AGAINST THE artificial light that poured in as Gavin climbed out of the shipping container, confirming my suspicions, and then listened to him leave with at least one other person. From the smell and the slight feeling of movement beneath me, I suspected that I was in a shipping container on a ship in port. Brian and Lancaster might both be here too if Gavin could be believed. I opened my hand where I had palmed the trident pin from Gavin's suit jacket while kissing him.

I applied the pin to the handcuffs at my wrist first and I had one hand free when I felt the vibrations. I pressed my cheek to the metal wall and felt the hum of a machine I didn't recognize. I had my ankles free now and I clipped Gavin's pin to the inside of my tweed vest. By the time I managed to break one of the legs off the chair I had been sitting in, I could faintly hear men's voices outside. Unless Gavin was coming back, the agents had arrived to pick up their hobbled prize. I needed to get out of here, but until I did, I could at least confound someone trying to get in. I used one of the handcuffs to hook around the bars that slid in place between the barn doors at the short end of the container.

The humming seemed to increase in pitch and move upwards, so I threw my satchel over my shoulder and pushed the empty wooden boxes in this container together against the wall, building myself a bit of a staircase up to the grain chute cut into the roof. I pressed up against the weighty rooftop opening with my shoulders, managed to open it about an inch and shoved the chair leg in to prop it open and allow me to look around. I could see the chain holding this rooftop door closed and shipping containers all around me, some stacked on top of each other and some already being examined by a pair of men holding flashlights. I ducked back down as the flashlights moved over my way, my heart beating so fast I had to remind myself to breathe. Even if Kell's men took me in, I had promised Michaels that I would deal with him. Maybe I should just let myself get taken in. That's when the machine I'd been hearing whirred above my head and lifted the shipping container to my left. I stifled a scream as it rotated the container and dropped it over the side of the ship into the water with a loud splash.

That did not seem to please the two men opening crates because they flicked off their flashlights and ducked where I could no longer see them. If containers were being dumped over the side of the boat, I no longer had the luxury of waiting for Kell's agents. Something had gone awry.

I pushed down on one end of the chair leg like a lever and with a grunt managed to crank it open enough to squeeze through the opening. I slid down the side of the container in the darkness, still holding my chair leg as a weapon.

"Thank God, Portia."

I looked up to see Brian Dawes staring down at me from the roof of another shipping container. "Come quick. It's your grandfather."

CHAPTER 38

"I'm fine. stop fussing," Sherlock Holmes said for the third time, batting at my hands.

"You collapsed, sir," Brian said from the front of the lorry. "Please let Portia take care of you."

"I do not need 'taking care of,'" the great detective grumbled as I wrapped a second blanket around him. His hand shot out of the layers of wool I was tucking around him to grab my wrist. He turned it over to view the red marks and his voice lowered to dangerous levels. "I will have his head for hurting you."

"He didn't, Grandfather, but he did confirm that he is the one bringing in the weapons for the Brits," I answered.

"Bought from the Swiss, of all people," Holmes put in. "Some locally manufactured, but a great many pulled from factories in Italy and Spain."

"We'll never bring him in on this, will we?" I said, sitting down next to him and sharing the blankets. "Brian?"

"I'm in pain, Portia, but I'm sober," he said turning the wheel with both hands and a wince. "And no, I agree. If Gavin is helping the coalition government and he has diplomatic status, we have no chance at all of arresting him."

"Our only hope is that he's double-crossing them at some stage of the process," Holmes said. "Something I need to look into through contacts of mine in those other countries."

"Was that you two dropping containers over the side of the ship?"

"Elementary mechanics," Holmes replied. "The machinery was right there and it was easy to identify which container you were in based on the arrangement of the containers and their movement as the sea churned, so we just picked one of the alternates to give you the time to escape. Everything was going according to plan when I just felt a little short of breath."

Brian wisely chose not to correct my grandfather, concentrating on the roads instead.

"What about Lancaster?" I asked. "Can we be sure he wasn't also being kept in a container?"

"Kell's men got to him before we could stop them," Holmes said, some colour coming back into his cheeks from the combination of my body heat and the blankets. "He's being taken, no doubt, to a place where he can be questioned away from the more legal eyes of Scotland Yard."

"I know a spot," I said grimly. "Brian, head towards Beans' place."

"Not a hospital?"

"No," said both Holmes and I simultaneously, to which Brian started grumbling under his breath about being blamed for the death of the greatest detective in the world.

"Thank you, my dear …," my grandfather started to say, but I interrupted him.

"I'm not taking you to a hospital because it's pointless," I said, rubbing at his arms. "You are an incorrigible patient. But I am asking you to go home to the country. You do better amongst your bees and fresh air and away from the stress of this city. It's why you left. It's why you stay away."

Holmes opened his mouth to argue, but I wouldn't let him. "The case is solved. Admit it. You and I both know what happened. This is but a long finale."

"There is still the matter of Gavin Whitaker and Trident and 'K.'"

"Which I am sure you can handle from the countryside — perhaps better if you'd finally had a phone line installed," I said. "Meanwhile, his immediate plans will be stymied by Brian and his colleagues at the Yard."

"Your faith in them astounds me," he admitted, glancing at the front of the lorry. "Present company excluded, of course, young man."

Brian actually smiled in spite of the situation, wiping at his forehead. "Though I still don't know why I called to have them evacuate the hotel. Someone had better explain it to me soon."

We ignored him, but shared a secret smile. "I weathered the explanations with my own Watson, my dear Portia," my grandfather said in a lower tone. "I admit to being too irascible to go through my methods again and again."

"Brian has the patience of a saint, much like John Watson, and he will wait," I said.

"I think he's through the worst of it," Holmes said, speaking so low I had to revert to reading his lips again. "But he will never be totally free of the call. We've talked about it at length and he understands what he stands to lose if he falls again. You must both stay vigilant. An addictive personality can have more than one vice."

"I will," I promised. "Thank you for talking to him. It's his faith in me that makes our partnership work."

"And why you don't need me," Holmes said, the slightest hint of hurt in his voice, something you could only discern if you knew him well.

"I do need you," I corrected him. "But so does my grandmother."

He turned his face away from me for a moment, and then glanced back. "The necktie?"

"No, the repeated application of royal jelly to your under-eyes. Did she make you wear that necktie?" I asked with a smile. "Her vanity is rubbing off on you, literally."

"It never works, you know," he said. "She's impossible. As am I."

"This could be the time 'it works,'" I answered, squeezing him tight, hoping against hope that I was right and that he and Irene Adler could find some peace in their tortured love story.

We drove Holmes to a shuttered schoolyard where Jenkins was waiting for him. I smiled at them both from the passenger side of the lorry, the legendary detective bundled in blankets and his resentful chauffeur, whose allegiance to my grandmother necessitated this brief alliance. Two men who loved Irene Adler and hated each other with every bit of their being.

"Are we going in the front door or the back?" Brian asked me as the Vauxhall 30 sped away into the night.

"Front," I answered, my eyes watching until the Vauxhall turned a corner and left my sight. "It's time Colonel Kell and I put all our cards on the table."

CHAPTER 39

I WALKED UP THE front steps of the five-storey building I had exited from the roof at the beginning of this adventure. A surprised escort formed around me and helped me get to my destination: a room much different than the one I had been interrogated in. It seemed to be the central hub of the building on the main floor and was behind two locked doors guarded by armed men dressed all in black. The large room was encircled by a few men at desks, corkboards with papers pinned all over them, blackboards of names, and a television set showing the front door of 10 Downing Street. That gave me pause. I'd never seen this level of live surveillance before using the camera and television technology. Imagine its usefulness in law enforcement. And in law evasion. My mind spun at the possibilities.

"What is it?" said Kell, not even looking up from his chair, facing away from the door. "I left express instructions not to be disturbed until you found the detective."

"Then I think we've satisfied your requirements," I said, my eyes on Lancaster, who was sporting one Hell of a black eye and sat in a wooden chair facing me. He tried to smile, but winced, the pain in his mouth stopping him. I couldn't help the glare directed at Kell when he finally turned at the sound of my voice.

"Miss Adams," Kell said, turning to face me. "This is a pleasant surprise. Here to confess?"

"I am," I replied. "But it would be best if I made the confession to you alone."

"Portia …," Lancaster started to say, speaking slowly out of his wounded mouth.

"I agree," Kell said, straightening his shoulders. "All the better to compare your stories at the end of this affair."

He emphasized the word *affair* and I fought against rolling my eyes at his childish attempt to embarrass us. He bullied his men and Lancaster out of the room.

"K, are you sure?" one of his men dared to ask.

"Are you seriously worried about the likes of her?" Kell answered. "Get out. And take Lancaster with you."

"It would be best if my associate was not harmed further," I said in a low voice. "Lest I be forced to retaliate."

"Are you threatening us with violence, Miss Adams?" Kell sputtered, looking me up and down, and doing that thing he did with his weapon, pulling aside his coat jacket to demonstrate its existence.

"My retaliation will be much worse," I promised, meeting the gaze of every man in the room. "Do not doubt me."

A full minute passed in shocked silence until one of the men reached out and closed the door behind them, eyes wide, leaving Kell and me alone in the large room.

"You have Holmes' arrogance," Kell said, folding his arms across his chest, his voice bouncing off the high ceiling. "That belief that superior intelligence trumps everything else. Loyalty. Country. Truth."

"An interesting list of what your priorities are," I said, taking a seat where Lancaster had been sitting. "Does your loyalty extend beyond your own limited view of who deserves it? Put another way, where was your loyalty to Lancaster?"

"Don't try and school me on Ian Lancaster," he spat. "That man has fouled every file he's been handed. The loss of Major Collins was just the ..."

"The murder of Major Collins was arranged by this office," I interrupted. "And I can prove it."

Kell turned three shades of red, but said nothing.

"The person who killed Major Collins and the informant became your most useful mole in the Irish movement," I said. "Their code name was Trident, not Major Collins. Lancaster admitted to me that their efforts had resulted in no useful information and suddenly, Collins dies and you're able to make headway for the first time in nearly a decade. They're still your most trusted agent — you sent them to meet with the prince when you suspected the O'Duffys were involved in the bombings."

Kell ground his teeth, but continued to silently stare at me, as if daring me to continue.

"Did you disavow Lancaster out of spite or because it aided your fictitious storyline of removing all agents from the area?" I asked, curious, but expecting no answer and receiving none. "It's Heddy that is the biggest question to me. Was she an agent or just a valuable pawn? It seems coincidental that she's in Ireland, and then she's with Major Collins, and then she's at Downing Street. When did she come on board with your group?"

"Heddy Collins is a patriot," Kell finally bit out. "Don't waste my time by repeating the rot you've been telling Lancaster about her being involved with the bombings. She would never."

"I agree. It sounds like that kind of attention would be her worst nightmare," I said. "Good thing we're talking to her in such a private location."

Kell followed my eye line to see Heddy Collins and Annie following Inspector Michaels through the previously closed door.

"Who the Hell do you think you are?" Kell managed to get out, his hand now massaging the butt of his gun. I was starting to think it was a bit of a safety blanket for the man rather than an actual threat of violence.

"Portia, I'm so glad to see you," Annie said, running to me as soon as she saw me. "Brian told me what happened. By the time I got to the fabric store, you were all gone."

"You were late, which I hope means that you found what I needed," I answered, returning her hug.

She grinned from ear to ear, handing me a bundle of paperwork. "Not just me."

"I contributed to that pile as well, Adams, so be sure to include me in your case file, won't you?" Michaels said, puffing around his usual cigar.

"Michaels, I might have known you were aiding and abetting these two," Kell said, jerking a chin at Lancaster, who had entered the room as well, pressing a bag of ice to his wounded chin.

"I have no idea who that is," Michaels said, escorting Heddy Collins into our midst and finding her a chair.

"Mrs. Collins, I will have you returned home as soon as I can locate my men," Kell said, speaking to the woman seated in our midst.

"That might take a few minutes," Michaels said. "Turns out your men have been dispatched to The Gore Hotel to round up the last of the missing bombs."

"Dispatched?" Kell repeated. "Dispatched by whom?"

"By His Royal Highness," Lancaster answered. "He did offer the full force of the British military, after all, and, upon hearing of this credible threat to the negotiators, pulled all your men out."

I sat down in front of Heddy Collins, who, remarkably, looked well-used to this level of hostility.

"Mrs. Collins, my name is Portia Adams," I said. "You've already met Annie and the inspector, and of course, you and Lancaster have known each other for years."

"Hello Heddy," Lancaster said. "I'm sorry you've been brought into this, but Portia would not be dissuaded."

Michaels and Kell both snorted at this understatement and then glared at each other.

"It's true. I'm very hard to wiggle off an idea once I've had it and I think I may have that in common with your daughter," I said, watching for a reaction from the woman with the unforgettable eyes.

"I do not have a daughter," she said finally, pressing her purse against her stomach like it could protect her. "Major Collins and I were only together for a few months."

She looked to Kell and Lancaster, who both nodded.

"A child from your first marriage," I corrected, "to Harold Digby."

This got a reaction. She clutched at her purse so tight her knuckles turned white.

"Val and Harold Digby," Annie said, opening the file on my lap. "Parents to Ilsa Digby, born 1919."

"And the marriage certificate of Valerie Zimmermann and Harold Digby, 1917," Michaels put in.

"Digby thought you left him because of the drink," I said, leaning forward "But I think you left because of the prejudice against you. I think you got fed up with being treated like an outsider and decided to leave your old miserable life behind. I don't know if you tried to make a go of it with your daughter and couldn't or if you planned to leave her at an orphanage

from the start, but at some point, you started over. You left
your old life and your old name behind and moved north where
no one would know you."

"No, no," Kell said, stepping forward to look at Annie's file.
"We looked into Heddy Weber when Collins revealed himself
to her. She was a refugee from the war."

"Heddy Weber fled Germany," I agreed, letting Annie flip pages
until she found the one she was looking for. "I suspect in the same
caravan that Valerie Zimmerman did."

"Did she die here or on the journey across the border, Val?"
Annie asked.

"She arrived in London, registered here as a refugee," I
answered when the woman seated in front of us would not.
"I suspect she died within a year of moving here, though. When
you moved away, you took her name with you so that Digby
couldn't find you.

"You're a survivor," I said with admiration. "Even when Major
Collins was killed, you pivoted, moved back to London with his
name and Lancaster's help, and then when Kell came to you with
an offer of employment, you threw Lancaster under the bus."

I looked up at Lancaster, seeing the hurt in his eyes, and
regretted that I would have to tell him what else had been done
to him in the service of his country.

"What has this to do with the bombs?" Kell broke in. "Even
if what you say is true, and Heddy Collins is actually Valerie
Zimmermann, surely you're not saying that she is behind the
bombings. Why would she target her place of work?"

"She wouldn't," I said. "But her daughter — who it turns out,
was smarter than any of you — found her out and came up with
a perfect revenge for being cast aside. First, she found her father
and then she ingratiated herself into the Collins family, perhaps

through the colonel, or perhaps through Alisha Collins." I looked to Michaels for this answer.

"Checked with the family and it sounds like Alisha was part of the Irish Feminist movement and brought home some friends, one of whom fits the description of young Ilsa," Michaels said.

"Right, so she found out about the bombs through her friend Alisha and suddenly she had an even better revenge than just outing the mother who abandoned her," I continued. "She stole the bombs and tried to use one to kill her father."

"Killing a good man by mistake," Michaels growled.

"Yes, and spraining her ankle, but leaving her father somehow alive," I said. "She was learning as she went. She tried again at Downing Street and at the college where you were taking language classes, Valerie. This must have been about when you suspected you were a target."

Annie sat down beside me to dig out the King's College student list and handed it to Kell while I spoke. Lancaster peered over her shoulder, shaking his head in disbelief.

"But what about Buckingham Palace?" Kell said. "Heddy … I mean … whomever this is, surely she wasn't at the palace."

Cognizant of the promise I had made I said, "Some of those phone calls were pranks, I'm sure, and some were overly paranoid citizens. No, I don't think Ilsa was targeting anyone but her parents."

"She was trying to kill us," said Valerie, making all of us jump a bit in surprise at the sound of her voice. "I had no choice."

"I think you did have a choice," I said, shaking my head. "But you're a survivor. After the Downing Street incident, you took the chance of seeking out some help from Trident, the spy you had helped elevate. They owed you for that, and trusted you, so you had them set up a meeting at Paddington Station with Ilsa through her Irish Feminist group. And you killed her there with the gun you'd carried over the border from Germany. A gun that I am guessing is in the bag you're clutching right now."

Valerie closed her eyes.

"You killed your own daughter?" Annie said. "Surely there was another way to maintain your anonymity."

"She wouldn't listen to reason. She wouldn't take money," Valerie answered, her eyes still closed, but crying now too. She handed the bag to me and I handed it to Michaels without opening it. "She wanted to see me destroyed. She said it was all that would make things right. It was her or me."

CHAPTER 40

"YOU DIDN'T KNOW THAT Digby would show up, or that he would kill himself," I said. "And I'm sure, as single-minded as you are about your own survival, that you didn't want to drag Lancaster back into this."

"What about the bombs at The Trifle?" Lancaster asked, his voice jagged with emotion as Michaels reached into Val's bag with a kerchief to pull out the Luger pistol.

"I believe those were arranged by Ilsa and her feminist friends to get rid of Éamon O'Duffy," I said. "When that failed, O'Duffy went looking for the culprits, found the bombs, and shipped them off to his brother in Sandwell for safe-keeping."

"But he didn't get them all," Lancaster pointed out. "What happened to the last of the bombs?"

"I think the man who can answer that has appeared," I said, pointing out Brian and Gavin as they walked towards us.

"Portia, how marvelous to see you again," Gavin said, taking me in his arms and kissing me on the forehead. "And Annie, you are a sight."

Annie just glared at him and I could tell Brian was doing his level best not to hurl himself at my ex, but Lancaster had no such compunction, grabbing Gavin by the collar. "You have some nerve walking in here, mate."

"Ah, Mr. Lancaster I presume," Gavin said, not even strug-gling in the spy's grip. "I hear you've been keeping our consulting detective quite busy. And I believe you've been working with my fiancée, Amélie."

Lancaster was still reeling from Valerie's admissions, but allowed Michaels to pry his hands off Gavin's collar.

"Colonel Kell, Amélie sends the thanks of the French govern-ment tonight for your success in averting the murder of the Austrian delegation, myself included. I believe you can be held personally responsible for saving the British people from the terrorists who have plagued them."

Kell took his hand off his gun for the first time in an hour, preening under Gavin's praise.

"With Amélie's help, the men of Scotland Yard were able to evacuate the hotel and recover the last of the bombs you've been searching for. Once Constable Dawes finished throwing up in the alleyway that is," Gavin said, his smile wide. "No fingerprints on the bombs, unfortunately, but the ladies of the Irish Feminist League are being detained at Scotland Yard, isn't that right, Constable?"

"They are," Brian admitted. "Along with Miss Amélie Blaise."

Gavin lost his grin for the first time in this interaction. "I'm sure I misunderstood. You mean Amélie is aiding you with the women she helped you arrest?"

"Amélie Blaise has been working both sides," I said, standing up to face Kell. "She was your agent in North Ireland, code-named Trident. And she was working for you and the French for some time. Then she made the mistake of falling in with Gavin Whitaker and, I must admit, myself."

Gavin stepped forward and Brian put his wounded hand on his shoulder, stopping him.

"She helped Gavin capture us at the fabric store," I said, unpinning the trident pin from the inside of my vest and handing it to Kell. "She's the one who retrieved the bombs after Ilsa was killed and sold some of them to various factions of the Irish rebellion — the O'Duffy family, the Feminist League. She switched to the Irish cause at some point in her employ. Or maybe she's a businesswoman, not a believer — you'll have to ask her that yourself. But she did keep a few bombs for her purposes tonight, even invited a few of her friends from the Feminist League to help her disrupt negotiations. Or at least, put some pressure on the negotiations so that Gavin here could increase his value. I wonder if she meant to kill everyone but you. Were you to be wounded? Or act the hero and save the PM?"

"That pin isn't evidence," Gavin hissed at me.

"You're saying her code name isn't Trident?" Lancaster challenged him.

"That's not …," Gavin started to say, and then corrected himself. "Her associations with the Secret Intelligence Service are her own. We don't discuss them and we certainly don't cross paths professionally. Colonel Kell, surely you can support me in this."

Kell was still holding out the pin in his palm like it might explode in his hand, but now he looked up — not at Gavin, but at me.

Brian handed me the bomb Gavin had put into my satchel. "You, of course, wiped down this bomb before leaving it in my satchel to give Kell the evidence he needed to hold me," I said. "But you were also smart enough to remove the firing pin so that I couldn't use it to escape before Kell's men found me — you're always one step ahead."

Brian nodded at Michaels, who pulled out a piece of paper

from Annie's file. "Inside Amélie Blaise's shoe heel we found one firing pin with her thumbprint on it. Fingerprints provided to us, most conveniently, by SIS"

"She is, after all, the professional in your relationship," I whispered in Gavin's ear. "You're the brains. You don't get your hands dirty."

He nodded slowly at me. "We'll have to call this a draw then," he whispered back before turning to Kell with shock on his face. "I have been as bamboozled as you, Colonel. I am appalled by the actions of the woman I love. What can I do to help ensure her imprisonment?"

CHAPTER 41

THE REUNIONS AT MY Baker Street apartment were ongoing.

My grandmother was waiting for me when we got home, hovering over the Coleson boys to make sure they were finishing their homework.

Heather stopped by and I spent an excruciating fifteen minutes not disclosing that I already knew she was engaged to the inspector before she finally got around to asking me to be her maid of honour. The reveal of the ring distracted my grandmother for a moment and she approved of the style — if not the expense — of the diamond, advising my cousin to change the setting before the wedding and promising to help her to find the right dress (whether she wanted the help or not).

The sons of Dr. Watson, my cousins and both doctors in their own right, came by to assess my recovery and chastise me for taking pills I didn't recognize.

My Baker Street Irregulars stood under my window until I stuck my head out, Ruby giving me a rare smile of approval when I proved I could hear her and speak to her again. I suggested they come back tomorrow morning for a catch-up over pancakes, my treat.

Irene Adler acted like she was still angry at me for my escape, but she allowed me to apologize at least and was sweet and forgiving to Brian when he apologized for not helping her when she asked. Mr. Coleson had been working hard fixing up the old townhouse, even now taking direction from Mr. Dawes on the banister they were replacing. Adler was still wearing minimal makeup and, after securing my promise to spend the next weekend with her, she left — no doubt to rejoin my grandfather, happy to report back that I was home safe.

"You did it," Jenkins said as he closed the car door behind my grandmother. "I never doubted it."

"Even when you were delivering Lancaster to the police?" I asked.

"Especially then," he said with a cocky grin. "The right motivation is a powerful thing."

"Your training is a powerful thing," I corrected him, giving him a kiss on the cheek. "I'll be back at your gym next week, I promise."

I watched them drive away, noticed the man standing across the street not really reading a newspaper, and walked over to him.

"Sir, surely you are done watching Baker Street at this point," I said, rubbing my hands together to keep warm. This spring was taking a long time to wrap things up and move on.

The man lowered the paper and looked over his shoulder at the car parked in the alleyway. Two men sat smoking in the front of the car facing forward with a piece of glass between us, the gathering smoke and glass obscuring them from my view. I sighed at the cloak-and-dagger dramatics and opened the back door to find Colonel Kell nursing a thermos between his knees.

"Trident was my best agent because no one would suspect a deaf black woman as being an agent," he said as soon as I was seated across from him. "It's what makes Lancaster good at his job as well."

"She was also brilliant and effective," I said, turning down the cap of tea he offered, despite the fact that I was chilled, and it smelled good. "And I'm glad Lancaster's skills have brought him back into the fold. He must be happy. Try not to waste his talents this time."

"You don't trust me," he said, taking back the cap and drinking from it. "I don't blame you. Lancaster said you warm slowly."

"Well, that was fun. I'd better get back to Annie and Brian; they're sure to be missing me," I said sarcastically, putting my hand on the door handle. "Please give Lancaster my regards."

"Miss Coleson is at this very moment being handed a new assignment that will take her overseas," Kell said, replacing the cap on his thermos. "One that I'd like you to join her on."

"You cannot be serious. I will not let you manipulate my best friend into serving you people," I said, sitting forward, my hands curling into fists.

"Miss Coleson will need somewhere else to be for a few months," Kell answered, looking away from me. "Her situation is one that will grow quite public and could ruin a good woman like her."

I gaped at him. He couldn't mean what he was implying. Especially if I hadn't noticed the signs. I would have noticed the signs.

"Besides, we have no intention of manipulating Miss Coleson," Kell said. "She's covering an important story for her paper, one that I assured her editor she would be kept safe while she covered it. I intend to keep that promise by asking you and Constable Dawes to go with her."

"I should have been clearer," I said. "If Annie needs help, then we will provide it. I have no intention of letting you manipulate any of us, K. We don't answer to you."

"No, but you do answer to king and country," said a voice I recognized from the radio. John Simon, the foreign secretary, slid the glass sideways between the front seat and back to speak to me directly. "And we're asking you to go. If not for your friend's reputation, then as a matter of national security."

I met Brian at the front door to Baker Street, his hand bound in a new bandage with a strange-smelling salve.

"Before you ask, a woman named Chen is here, said she was your friend, and bound my hand like this before I could do anymore than ask her nephew to translate what she was saying," he said, opening the door wider so I could see them in the front hallway. Chen was loudly advising Mrs. Dawes on her husband's vision issues, using poor Lin as their translator. Luckily, he was halfway through a plate of cookies so he didn't need rescuing and I followed Brian up the stairs to my flat, Nerissa right behind us.

Brian collapsed into my couch with a sigh, flexing his bound hand, my bloodhound at his feet. "Thank God all that's over," he said. "What's in the box?"

Instead of answering I sat down next to him, wiggling my toes so that they were under my warm dog and handing him the box I'd just been given by Kell.

"A gun?" Brian said, looking from the opened box to me. "Portia, if this is about Whitaker, we will catch him. He's addicted to power. This time he had a scapegoat, but next time we will nail him to the wall. We needn't ..."

I interrupted him with a shake of my head. "That's my father's Colt, Brian. I'd recognize it anywhere from the melted mark on the butt. It was made by my mother's curling iron. She put it down on her wardrobe and the gun was hidden under some letters. The letters caught fire, but the gun suffered this damage."

"Did you bring it with you from Toronto?"

"No, I thought it lost to my step-father's gambling," I said. "Sold to a local pawn broker for a few dollars."

"But … how?" Brian asked, holding the weapon aloft.

"Somehow, my father's gun is involved in the attempted assassination of a member of the Canadian parliament, a Mr. William King," I replied, taking the gun from Brian gingerly, "and we must find out how."

ACKNOWLEDGEMENTS

This fourth Portia Adams book has been a long time coming for many reasons, not the least of which was the loss of my fabulous first publishers, Fierce Ink Press, which had to close its doors in 2017.

It is only through the faith and support of people like Shelagh Rogers and Marc Côté that I was able to continue Portia's journey on the page and I will be forever grateful for that.

Thank you to all the fans and readers who pursued me at book events, chased me on social media and basically willed this book into reality. I will never be able to thank you enough for your love and support. I only hope I can continue to be a part of your bookshelves virtual and physical alike.

The publishing team at Cormorant helped me grow Portia's story from her YA origins to the adult force of nature she is now.

Special thanks to my husband, Jason, and my daughter, Kenzie, for their love and support.

There have been so many teachers and librarians who have supported my books since the first day of their publication, and I will never be able to repay them for that. This is especially true of Zelia Tavares and Kamla Rambaran who worked with me this year on a mystery-writing workshop that their grade six classes knocked out of the ballpark. That workshop could not have happened without the Royal Ontario Museum's Kiron Muckherjee's brilliant help.

To the indie bookstores like Book City on St. Clair W, Queen Books on Queen west, Another Story in Roncy and the Mysterious Bookshop in NYC, who continue to carry my books and speak of my characters to your readership, thank you!

The Bootmakers of Toronto, Sisters in Crime, FOLD, and the Crime Writers of Canada have become dear friends in addition to being ardent supporters and I am so pleased to have found them.

The Internets continue to be very kind to me in this process, so I am very thankful for my writers' groups (especially #write-o-rama on Facebook) and for all the folks who follow and comment on my blog and who invited me onto their websites for the blog tour.

Finally, thank you, dear reader, for buying The Detective and the Spy! If you get a chance, let me know what you think, on my blog, www.angelamisri.com and please do post a review on Amazon, Goodreads or Chapters-Indigo.

We acknowledge the sacred land on which Cormorant Books operates. It has been a site of human activity for 15,000 years. This land is the territory of the Huron-Wendat and Petun First Nations, the Seneca, and most recently, the Mississaugas of the Credit River. The territory was the subject of the Dish With One Spoon Wampum Belt Covenant, an agreement between the Iroquois Confederacy and Confederacy of the Ojibway and allied nations to peaceably share and steward the resources around the Great Lakes. Today, the meeting place of Toronto is still home to many Indigenous people from across Turtle Island. We are grateful to have the opportunity to work in the community, on this territory.